Arisa Palmer

Brenda Bellingham

DROWNING IN SECRETS

cover art by
Ginette Beaulieu

Scholastic Canada Ltd.
Toronto, New York, London, Sydney, Auckland

Scholastic Canada Ltd.
175 Hillmount Road, Markham, Ontario, Canada L6C 1Z7

Scholastic Inc.
555 Broadway, New York NY 10012, USA

Scholastic Australia Pty Limited
PO Box 579, Gosford, NSW 2250, Australia

Scholastic New Zealand Ltd.
Private Bag 94407, Greenmount, Auckland, New Zealand

Scholastic Ltd.
Villiers House, Clarendon Avenue, Leamington Spa,
Warwickshire CV32 5PR, UK

Canadian Cataloguing in Publication Data

Bellingham, Brenda, 1931 –
 Drowning in secrets

ISBN 0-590-12487-0

I. Title.

PS8553.E468D76 1998   jC813'.54   C98-930686-0
PZ7.B34Dr 1998

Copyright © 1998 by Brenda Bellingham
All rights reserved.

No part of this publication may be reproduced or stored in a retrieval
system, or transmitted in any form or by any means, electronic,
mechanical, recording, or otherwise, without written permission of
the publisher, Scholastic Canada Ltd., 175 Hillmount Road,
Markham, Ontario, Canada L6C 1Z7. In the case of photocopying or
other reprographic copying, a licence must be obtained from
CANCOPY (Canadian Reprography Collective), 6 Adelaide Street
East, Suite 900, Toronto, Ontario, M5C 1H6.

5 4 3 2 1   Printed in Canada   8 9/9 0 1 2/0

For my beloved granddaughters:
Katelyn and Megan

A woman, dressed in white, floats a little below the surface of the water, the skirt of her dress gently lifting and falling, her skin bone-white, her legs caught by the weeds. Terrified, she stretches up her white arms for help.

Help her! Get her out! Now, before it's too late! Chloe screams.

She reaches through the water, but the woman's hands slip out of her grasp. Again she tries. And again. Each time she fails. The woman will sink soon, down, down into the weeds, never to escape. To reach her, Chloe will have to dive into the water, but she can't bring herself to do it. What if she becomes entangled in the weeds, too, bound by their unyielding tendrils, unable to move?

Something brushes against her. The woman's arms and legs weave through her own. Chloe pushes the woman away, but the body floats back toward her. There is no fear in the woman's eyes now, no appeal for help.

Chloe is too late.

Sobbing with guilt, her arms flailing against the sheet that has fallen over her face, she wakes. She cannot recall the drowned woman's features any more than she can recall the face of her own dead mother. But dreamers do not need the evidence of their senses. They have a darker, deeper way of knowing . . .

Chapter One

For someone running away from home — sort of — she was doing it all wrong. Chloe Griffiths frowned at the huge suitcase beside her feet. Even without her hand-luggage the suitcase immobilized her. Like a ball and chain, she thought. Other kids her age walked through the bus station with all their gear loaded into bulging backpacks. Free. While she looked like some loser. And another thing — she needed to pee. Probably the suitcase wouldn't even fit inside one of those cubicles, and she couldn't just leave it here.

Glancing behind, she caught the eye of an older woman. These days you weren't supposed to say "old"; senior citizen was the correct term. Not that it altered anything. Why were people afraid to call things by their real names? Like Dad. Why did he say, "after we lost your mother," as if she were a package they'd left somewhere? Why couldn't he say, "after your mother died," or, even, "after your mother drowned," when he mentioned it at all? It

1

was like he thought if you didn't talk about it, you could pretend it hadn't happened.

The woman smiled at her. Maybe I could ask her to watch my suitcase, Chloe thought. Joyce was always telling Jason and Matthew, "If you get lost, look for a woman who looks like a grandma to help you."

You had to be careful about talking to strangers in bus stations, though. Places like these harboured creepy characters — human cockroaches who crawled out of the walls to prey on young runaways. They'd offer a bed and friendship, but everyone knew those were just code words for drugs and prostitution. Chloe understood why the runaways fell for it. They felt like pieces of abandoned luggage, just waiting to be claimed. She imagined the cockroaches smoking cigars and wearing loud jackets, but that was wrong. They'd be disguised as regular people, the better to trap anyone naïve enough to believe them. But surely they wouldn't be disguised as grandmothers.

"Smile, Chloe," Joyce had told her when she was still young enough to hide behind her or Dad. "Even if you feel shy, a smile can't hurt you."

She returned the woman's smile.

"This is the worst part of a trip, I always think," the woman said. "Standing in line. Bus stations, airports, they're all the same."

Chloe smiled again. The ice was broken. Chalk one up for Joyce.

As if in answer to her name, Chloe's stepmother came rushing toward her through the bus terminal, with Jason and Matthew running at her heels.

Chloe's relief quickly changed to misgiving. Saying good-bye to the little guys had proved to be the hardest part of leaving. Now she'd have to go through it again, and she hated making a fool of herself in public.

"I had to stop by the bank," Joyce said, panting, "Thank goodness we're in time."

For what? Chloe thought. To try and talk me into going back? It won't work, Joyce. I'm sixteen. I have every right to know my mother's closest relatives. If Dad can't accept that, tough.

She'd expected him to give in — at least follow her to the bus station to make sure she was okay, not leave it to Joyce, whose usual policy was to keep out of fights between her and Dad. Not that they'd ever had one this serious before. Usually he wasn't this unreasonable. He took time to explain his point of view and then left her to make her own decision. Come to think of it, she often ended up seeing things his way. But not this time.

Joyce fumbled in her purse and took some bills out of her wallet. "Take this," she said.

"I don't need it, thanks," said Chloe, raising her chin. "I have my own money."

"It isn't much. And you don't have to spend it, knuckle-head. It's for emergencies."

No point arguing. She took the money.

"And, Chloe, if you run into trouble, for pete's sake phone. If you're too proud to ask your father for help, ask me."

Since when had Joyce turned into such a worrier? It wasn't like her. Dad storming, Joyce fussing! Who wouldn't be suspicious about why they were trying to stop her from visiting her mother's relatives?

Jason tugged on her shirt. "Don't go, Chloe. Please." He was the serious one of her little half-brothers, old for his seven years.

Matthew, younger and more rambunctious, wound his arms around Chloe's leg. "I'm going to hang on so you can't go."

Between them they brought a lump to her throat. "What's with you two?" she said. "It's not the end of the world. I'm going to visit my grandma and Aunt Roseanna for two or three weeks. You like to visit *your* gran."

"Why can't we come?" demanded Matthew.

"You're too little."

"Why did Dad get so mad at you?" asked Jason, his eyes suspicious.

"Boys," Joyce warned. "Stop bugging Chloe." Lowering her voice she said, "Chloe, are you sure about this? It's not just a face-saving gesture, is it, because your dad said you couldn't go? I mean, he loves you, Chloe, and even if they are your mother's relatives, you don't know anything about these people."

"And whose fault is that?" Chloe said. "His!" It still made her hot to think about it. Just because her mother had died didn't make her family dead too. Until her sixteenth birthday, her father had let her think they'd lost touch and didn't care about her. Then he'd given her Aunt Anna's letters, one for every birthday and Christmas. Letters he'd been keeping from her for years.

"Joyce, Aunt Anna's letters sounded totally normal. She didn't try to run Dad down, or anything. She didn't even mention him." Come to that, she didn't mention my mother either, Chloe thought, just told me about herself and Gran and what they'd been doing — almost like pen-pal letters. Except, thanks to Dad, I never had a chance to reply. "This is something I have to do," she said. "Anna is my mother's identical twin, remember. If anyone can tell me what really happened to my mother, she can."

Joyce sighed. "There's no mystery about it. Your mother went out sailing alone, and drowned. Such things happen, Chloe."

"So why did Dad keep Anna's letters a secret until now? Look, Joyce, he even made Anna write him in care of that Vancouver lawyer. I can't believe he wouldn't even give her his address."

"I can't answer for your dad, Chloe, but I don't think he and Anna like one another very much. People don't always get along with their in-laws. I think he really told you all there is to know."

Or all he *wants* me to know, thought Chloe. If it's all so simple and straightforward, why does he get uptight if I try to talk about my mother? As if he still hasn't got over her even though he's been married to Joyce for eight years.

"I still want to meet my mother's twin," Chloe said. "What's so odd about that?" She wouldn't even say the other reason, the reason that preyed on her mind: She couldn't remember anything about her mother. Not how she looked, not what they had done together, not a single, solitary thing. Her dad's explanation that people often had no memories of their early childhood just didn't cut it. The memories were there, somewhere, locked away. She was sure of it. Otherwise she wouldn't have the recurring nightmare that haunted her, but explained nothing. There must be a reason for this mental block, and maybe Anna knew what it was. Anna and her mother had been identical twins, so seeing Anna would be almost like seeing her mother again. Surely that would awaken the memories.

"Okay, Chloe, it's clear your mind's made up," Joyce said. "But remember, if you run into a problem, I'm here for you."

Joyce's concern almost made Chloe choke up, so she turned it into a joke. "Since you're here for me, could you watch my luggage while I go to the can? I'm desperate."

Joyce nodded. "Off you go."

Matthew had been leaning against Chloe's leg, watching the people in the bus station, but as soon as she moved he fastened his arms around her legs again. She unhooked him and fled to the washroom. It was hard, leaving the little kids.

This wasn't your usual kind of trip and the boys knew it. Chloe frowned at herself in the mirror while she washed her hands and waited for the air machine to dry them. Why was Dad so set against her going? Why hadn't he let her keep in touch with her aunt and grandmother? "My company moved us around a lot and I'm a terrible letter writer," he'd said. "I just kind of lost touch." She didn't believe him. Tears of anger sprang to her eyes when she remembered his lame excuse. He was forcing her to take off, with his refusal to tell her the truth.

When she got back, the line for the Vancouver bus had moved up. So had Joyce and the boys, with Chloe's suitcase.

"They're starting to board," Joyce said. "Chloe, are you sure — "

"I'm sure."

Joyce nodded. Matthew and Jason, solemn-eyed, came with Chloe as far as they were allowed, then said good-bye.

Their hugs almost made her cry again. Luckily the driver was demanding tickets, giving information.

"Leave your suitcase beside the bus," he said. "I'll load it."

She had no time to cry. Still hoping that her dad might turn up, she found a window seat and stared outside. She hated leaving him like this, with things all wrong between them. In spite of their fight, she still loved him. If only he'd say he was sorry, then she would, too — although she'd still go to Salmon Arm.

The older woman who had been behind her in the line sat beside Chloe and took an air pillow out of her huge bag. "Might as well get comfortable," she said, starting to blow up the pillow. "It's a long trip. I'm staying with friends in Salmon Arm for a couple of nights, then going on to Vancouver to see my new grandson."

Reluctantly, Chloe turned from the window. It was too late for Dad to come now. The driver was in his seat, getting ready to leave. Above the throbbing of the engine he made a few announcements over the intercom about bathrooms and stops. Outside, metal doors clanged and men called to one another. The bus's air brakes hissed and the driver slowly backed it out of the loading bay.

"How far are you going?" the woman asked.

"Salmon Arm. My aunt and grandmother live near there."

Joyce and the boys were walking alongside the bus, looking for her. Chloe waved frantically, but they stared blankly back.

"They can't see you," the woman said. "The glass is treated so we can see out but people can't see in."

Disappointed, Chloe leaned back in her seat and watched the stores and high, glass office buildings of Edmonton pass by. It was weird seeing them from the bus, as if they were no longer familiar, but part of an alien city. Then they were crossing the river to the south side. How would she feel when she came back? Like the same person, or different? What exactly would she have found out?

Whatever it is, it would be better to know the truth, she told herself firmly. Maybe then I can do something about it instead of only imagining what's behind that horrible nightmare. And those panic attacks lately.

She shut her eyes and let her head fall back.

Why can't I remember my mother? Was it somehow *my* fault she died . . . ? Is *that* what Dad's trying to hide from me . . . ?

Chapter Two

The feeling of *déjà-vu* was so strong that it stopped Chloe in mid-sentence. It's happened before, she thought. Just like this. She'd stood on this same garden path, its slabs of silk-smooth rock settled by time into the ground. Faced the same front door, startlingly white against the soft green of the cedar siding, with that fan-shaped window of amber-coloured panes set above it. Caught a glimpse of sparkling sunlight on the lake between the towering firs that surrounded the house. Inside, the hall would be filled with shafts of light.

Anna, her hand on the knob of the front door, paused. "Chloe?"

Aunt Anna must have been surprised by her sudden silence. All the way from the bus station in Salmon Arm, where Anna had picked her up, Chloe had talked almost non-stop. Chatterbox, her dad called her. Motor Mouth, teased her friends. But everybody did it, didn't they? Streams of words rushing over what they were really thinking and feeling. She couldn't help it if she was better at it than most people.

"I'll just get rid of my parcels then I'll give you a hand," Anna said.

"It's okay, thanks. I can manage." Again Chloe regretted her huge suitcase. Aunt Anna must think she meant to stay forever. She hitched her carry-all higher on her shoulder, picked up the suitcase and lugged it to the front door.

From the hallway Anna called softly, "Hello-o, Marg. We're home."

A door opened and a pleasant looking middle-aged woman came down the hall. She smiled at Chloe.

"Marg," Anna said. "This is my niece, Chloe Griffiths. Chloe, this is Marg Wickel, a neighbour, and friend."

"Hi," said Chloe.

"Glad to meet you, Chloe," Marg replied.

"Is everything all right?" Anna asked, a hint of anxiety in her hushed voice.

"Just fine," said Marg. "Your mother's still napping. I'll be off home now that you're back, Anna. All right? See you, Chloe."

While she waited for Anna to show Marg out, Chloe looked around. From the hallway a flight of stairs led to an upper floor. The hall and stairway were dim, but through the fan-shaped window above the front door, shafts of sunlight slanted across the hall to settle into a golden pool on the hardwood floor. "I knew it," she said, smiling.

"I'm sorry," Anna said, coming in. "I didn't quite

11

catch what it was you — "

"It's totally weird," Chloe said. "As soon as I got here, I felt it. As if I'd been here before, in this house I mean. I've walked up the garden path, come through the front door and stood in the hall, just like we're doing now. I knew it would be filled with golden light from that window over the door. It's what they call *déjà-vu*, isn't it?" she ended, breathless with excitement.

Anna hesitated, as if unsure how to answer. "But, Chloe, dear, you *have* been here before."

"I have? When?"

Anna picked up a couple of grocery bags and headed for the kitchen. Chloe seized another bag and followed her.

Anna began putting away the groceries. "You used to spend your summers here, you and your mother. Your dad joined us on weekends and for summer holidays. You don't remember?"

"No," Chloe admitted. "Not at all." She wished Anna would keep still and look at her.

At last Anna closed the fridge door. "Well, you were very young, so it's not surprising. I'm sorry to spoil the *déjà-vu* theory. Seeing the house again probably brought a couple of buried memories to the surface."

"There go my hopes of being psychic," Chloe said. But she really didn't mind. It was a good start. Memories were what she was after, not psychic abilities. She hoped she hadn't hurt Anna's feelings by admitting she'd forgotten her. "No wonder I felt I knew you at the bus station," she went on. "As soon as I met you, you seemed so comfortable to be with, somehow. Like an old friend."

Anna's face flushed. "I'm so glad, Chloe. I'd hoped we'd be friends."

Anna wanted to hug, Chloe could tell, but was holding back, not sure it would be welcome. Chloe took matters into her own hands and hugged Anna.

As they broke apart, Anna asked, "Chloe, are you sure you don't remember being here?"

"Certain." Chloe frowned. "And Dad never mentioned it."

"No, I guess not." A shadow passed over Anna's face, then it was gone and she smiled. "Come upstairs and I'll show you your bedroom. You can freshen up while I check on your grandma."

"Aunty Anna, I was hoping you'd tell me more about my mother and how she died," Chloe said. "Dad hasn't told me much about that either."

Anna grabbed Chloe's bag and headed upstairs. She had the pale skin that went with red hair, and even from the back Chloe could see her neck flush. "We'll have lots of time to talk while you're here," Anna said. "Right now I have to see to your grandma. She gets frightened if she wakes up and thinks she's alone. By the way, Chloe. You don't have to call me Aunt or Aunty. It makes me feel like an old Victorian lady. Anna will do just fine."

Lugging her suitcase, Chloe followed Anna upstairs. The story of my life, she thought, nobody ever wants to tell me anything. It's like there's some sort of conspiracy to keep me from finding out the truth.

Chapter Three

"You'll find the house takes a bit of getting to know, because the layout's sort of peculiar," Anna said as she led Chloe along an upstairs hallway. "You see, it started out as a summer cottage. Then we gradually started spending more time here and your grandfather added bits as we needed them. Eventually it became our permanent home."

To her disappointment, Chloe did not remember the upstairs. The house seemed to have numerous corners and little flights of stairs, including another, rather narrow, staircase. "Where does that go?" she asked.

"Not anywhere, really. Before he passed away, your grandfather planned to add to the house. I'm afraid he only had time for the stairs, though. Come on, your bedroom's just around here."

Chloe's bedroom was up a few steps at the end of the hall and at the back of the house, overlooking the lake. A double bed with a white bedspread, flanked by two small, square, antique wicker night tables painted white, took up almost all the space. A pine dresser stood against the wall facing the foot of the bed, and on the same wall was a cupboard-like closet. Two small stained-glass windows were set high into the wall behind the bed.

Anna stood back, watching Chloe's face. "Is it all right?"

"It's great!" cried Chloe. "I love it."

Anna turned pink with pleasure. "I hoped you'd like it. It used to be my room. Your mother had the one next door. Now I've made it into a den. I sleep downstairs to be near your grandmother."

Chloe's attention had been caught by a drawing, tinted with watercolour, hanging over the head of the bed. At first she thought it was of a young woman looking at herself in a mirror, then she realized it was a double portrait. "This is of you and my mother, isn't it?" The young women were smiling, as if they shared some secret joke. They had delicate colouring and small, pointed faces surrounded by a lot of frizzy red hair. "Which one is my mother?" Then, before Anna could answer, "No, don't tell me. Let me guess. This one. Right?"

Anna shook her head. "Look closely," she said. "You'll see we're wearing gold necklaces with our names written in gold wire. Roselinda and Roseanna. Cute, eh? After awhile even our parents got tired of two Roses in the house. Your mother called herself Roz, and me Anna, and the names stuck."

Chloe felt hot with shame. She couldn't even recognize her own mother! What must Anna think? "I've only ever seen one photo of my mother," she said defensively. "It's in a locket so it's very small. Dad gave it to me." After I bugged the life out of him, she could have added, and him insisting it was the only one he'd kept.

"You aren't the first one to be confused," Anna said. "We were identical twins, remember? Even our parents had trouble keeping us straight. It doesn't matter."

But it *does* matter, thought Chloe. I should remember my mother — something, anything. There shouldn't be a total blank. And surely there couldn't be any better key for unlocking her memory than this portrait. She felt as if she had taken the first test of her self-imposed mission, and failed.

She knelt on the bed to get a closer look, and stared until the image was etched into her brain. "Who painted this?"

"Your father. See the initials in the corner: O.G. — Owen Griffiths."

"You're kidding!"

"I think he was intrigued by the challenge of painting identical twins," Anna said. "Roz and I were what they call mirror-image twins. For example, she was right-handed, while I'm a lefty. Her right profile was more like my left — or so we were told. That's what gave your father the idea of painting us as if we were looking into a mirror."

Chloe heard a flatness in Anna's voice that suggested she was trying to sound objective, like the guides who showed you around the art gallery.

"I didn't know he could paint like this," she said.

"Oh, I know he can draw — cartoons and his advertising stuff — but not portraits."

"He used to be a good portrait artist when he was young," Anna said, her tone still neutral. "I expect he hasn't time now, what with his job and a family."

"Maybe that's why he encourages me," Chloe said. "He told me to forget a summer job and take an art course. I like painting, but I really want to be an actress. I told you that in my letter, didn't I? And then there's band. I play the clarinet and I kind of enjoy it."

Anna smiled and Chloe realized that her mouth was running away with her again. She broke off her monologue and went to the window. "What a view. I can see the whole lake."

"Not really," Anna said. "The Shuswap has four arms and numerous bays. That's what makes it so interesting. We're on the Salmon Arm. That narrow passage up there leads to the Seymour Arm. Remind me to show you a map later." On the way out she paused in the doorway, blushing, her eyes bright. "I can't tell you how glad I am to see you again, Chloe. As soon as you're organized, come down and say hello to your grandmother."

Before Chloe could answer, Anna was gone. She's kind of nervous, Chloe thought, as if I scare her for some reason.

She turned back to study the portrait of her mother. "Mother?" she whispered. "Is that what I used to call you?" Or did I say Mom, or Mommy? Even Mama? Weird not to remember. There was so much she didn't know. She waited, hoping that the portrait might yet spark some feeling of recognition. Eventually she gave up and climbed off the bed.

Better get on with unpacking. It might seem rude to hang around in her room, and she wanted to make a good impression on her first visit. Only it wasn't her first. Why hadn't her dad told her? She glanced back at the portrait. He hadn't told her about that, either. After all these years, what was it about her mother that he still found too disturbing to talk about?

That was the trouble with him. He held things close to himself, like a man clutching a pain, refusing to let anyone help, not even his daughter who loved him with all her heart. Angrily, she swiped at a tear. She wouldn't cry. What was done was done. She was sixteen now — old enough to make her own decisions. She had every right to know her relatives, especially her mother's twin sister.

And I don't care how Dad feels about Anna, Chloe thought. I really like her. But she shouldn't wear her hair pulled back like that. It makes her look severe, as if she's trying not to look attractive.

"Chlo-eee." Anna's voice floated up the stairs. "Is everything all right?"

"Just coming." Chloe let the lid of her suitcase drop and ran down the stairs.

Anna was waiting at the door of the front room. "I didn't mean to rush you," she said.

Chloe made a mental note to slow down. Miss Perpetual Motion, Joyce called her, and Joyce and Dad were used to kids. In this house, a sixteen-year-old girl might be like a stray dog. They'd want to be kind to it, but they might find it a bit of a nuisance. With luck, though, they'd grow fond of it, if it behaved well.

At the bottom of the stairs Chloe hung back, but Anna put her arm around Chloe's shoulders and guided her into the room.

A tall, frail-looking lady sat in a low chair near the fireplace. She leaned forward, resting her weight on the handle of a black cane, and gazed into the empty fireplace as though flames danced there. She had high cheekbones and a slightly hooked nose, like the beak of an eagle. She glanced up and Chloe saw that her blue eyes were deeply set. Her hair was silver. She's beautiful, thought Chloe. All those lines. I wonder if I could draw her.

Anna led Chloe forward. "Mother, this is — "

"Roz!" Grandma Kenyon cried. "Oh, my darling Roz." Leaning on her cane she struggled to her feet, then, dropping the cane, she held out her arms. "You've come back. I always knew you would." Tears ran down her cheeks. Her shoulders heaved with sobs and her body swayed.

Afraid that her grandmother would fall, Chloe stepped into her waiting arms. Her grandmother hugged her close, stroking her hair, all the time calling her "little Roz."

"I'm not Roz," Chloe tried to say, "I'm Chloe." But she could hardly breathe, let alone talk, she was pressed so tightly against her grandmother. She couldn't believe that someone who looked so frail could be so strong. But her grandmother's strength gradually ebbed. She fell back into her chair, almost pulling Chloe on top of her. Chloe stood up and got her breath back.

Anna knelt beside her mother and took her hand. "Mother, this isn't Roz, it's Chloe. I told you she was coming for a visit." Anna's voice trembled and the colour in her cheeks and neck came and went. She patted Grandma Kenyon's hand and tried to steady her own voice. "Chloe was only five the last time we saw her, but now she's all grown up. She's just had her sixteenth birthday. You helped me pick out a birthday card. Do you remember? She looks just like Roz at that age. No wonder you got mixed up."

Grandma Kenyon began to look as if she understood.

On the way from the bus station Anna had warned Chloe that Grandma Kenyon sometimes got confused. She'd had a series of strokes that had left her with a limp and some loss of memory.

Relieved that her grandmother seemed to be getting it together, Chloe smiled. "Hello, Grandma," she said. "I'm really glad to meet you at last."

Grandma Kenyon's sad expression suddenly changed. Shocked, Chloe backed away. Was it fear or anger that contorted her grandmother's face?

"No!" Grandma Kenyon shouted. "Go away. I don't want you here. You'll only cause trouble. So much unhappiness. All because of you. I can't stand any more of it." Sobbing as if her heart would break, she hunched her shoulders and buried her head in her hands.

Chapter Four

Chloe fled to her bedroom. It *was* her fault! Something she'd done *had* caused her mother's death. That must be why Dad had always refused to talk about it. He'd been trying to protect her.

She grabbed her suitcase, flung the lid open and began to throw in the clothes she'd unpacked. Now that she knew for sure, she'd go home and confront him. Make him tell her.

"Chloe!" Anna stood in the doorway, her face as white as porcelain. "What are you doing?"

"Packing. I can't stay here, not now. Not after what Grandma said. I'll catch the next bus out of here."

Anna put her hand to her forehead and briefly closed her eyes, as though the scene downstairs had given her a headache. "I'm sorry. It's my fault. I should've . . . I couldn't . . . I didn't foresee how Mother would react." She sank down on the side of the bed.

Chloe went on tossing clothes into the suitcase.

"It's not your fault," she said. "Dad was right. I never should've come."

The mention of Owen seemed to rouse Anna's anger. She caught hold of Chloe's wrist so that she was forced to stop packing. "He's *not* right! When you were little, you were as close to me as my own child. We have every right to get to know one another again." Her voice had a catch in it. "Please stay."

"How can I?" Chloe asked. "Grandma doesn't want me here. She hates me."

Anna released Chloe's wrist and stood up, her fingers fidgeting. She had slender hands, the skin pale, almost transparent, showing the pattern of blue veins. "I wish you could remember your grandmother from before . . . "

Before what? Chloe wondered. Before I did something awful to my mother?

" . . . before her stroke," said Anna. "By tomorrow she'll have forgotten this ever happened. Give her, give us both, another chance. Can you, Chloe?"

"I don't know." She looked Anna straight in the eye. "Before I decide, you've got to tell me. What did Grandma mean when she said it was my fault?"

Anna, frowning, shook her head. "She didn't mean it." As she frequently did, she hesitated. "Seeing you reminded her of Roz and gave her a shock. You brought back her memory of Roz's — well, tragedy."

Tragedy! Another false word for death. "That wouldn't make her hate me," she said. Restless, she went to the window before she turned back to face

Anna. "You don't have to hide the truth. I've suspected for some time that it was my fault my mother died. I killed her, didn't I?"

"No!" cried Anna, jumping up. "Where on earth did you get an idea like that? Nothing could be farther from the truth. Nothing." She twisted her hands in agitation. "How could you have killed your mother?"

"I don't know," Chloe said. "I have these dreams . . . Anyway, I mean to find out."

Anna stared at her hands for what seemed ages, as if considering what she should say, then she took a deep breath. "Sit down, Chloe." She waited while Chloe settled herself, cross-legged, in the middle of the bed, then perched on the end.

"There's something you should know. Before she died, Roz had been sick for some time, but none of us really realized it. She fell into terribly black moods, locking herself in her room for hours at a time. We blamed my father's sudden death for the change in her personality — she adored him, and he was so proud of her. She was so gifted, Chloe — not only athletic, a good sailor and swimmer, but artistic, too. She took Father's death really hard. Finally, when you were five, we had to face the fact that Roz was suffering from a severe mental illness. Owen insisted she go to hospital for treatment."

Before Chloe could ask the question, Anna answered it. "No, he wasn't trying to get rid of her, or anything unpleasant like that. Mother and I agreed with him. It wasn't an easy decision, but it had to be made."

Anna stood up and gazed into space, at times squeezing her hands together, at others fidgeting with her dress. "While your mother was in hospital, you stayed here with your grandmother and me."

"Dad never told me."

"No. I suppose not. Your father never was one to talk about difficult things. Anyway," Anna went on, "Roz hated being in the hospital. One day she managed to slip out. Shortly after, the hospital alerted us that she'd gone. Then I discovered her sailing dinghy was missing from the boathouse. Father had given it to her and she loved it. I thought she'd gone sailing to calm herself, to celebrate getting away and coming home — that sort of thing. But later that day the police found it drifting on the lake, with her clothes neatly folded and a note saying she intended to take her own life." She glanced down at Chloe, then gazed back off into space again. "Her body was never found."

Chloe was glad she was sitting on the bed. She suddenly felt trembly and weak. This was a total surprise. "You mean . . . she committed suicide?"

"That's certainly how it looked, although the official verdict was 'missing, presumed drowned.' But one thing is certain, Chloe. Whatever happened to Roz had nothing to do with you. You couldn't possibly have killed her. You must believe that." Anna's face was drawn, all the little lines suddenly magnified, as if she'd grown older while they talked.

"I'm sorry," Chloe said. "I shouldn't have made you talk about it. I — I never suspected . . . I wish Dad had told me."

"After the police enquiries were over," Anna went on, "I wanted to keep you here with us, but one day your father just took off with you, without telling us he was going. We haven't seen you from that day to this. The only communication we had with him was through his lawyer. Did he tell you that?"

"Hmmm?" Chloe had hardly listened to the rest of what Anna had said. Now she forced herself to focus. "Not — not until a few months ago. He didn't tell me my mother had been in a mental hospital either. He only told me she'd drowned — an accident, he said." She frowned, puzzled. "I wonder why he didn't tell me the truth."

"Because there's such a stigma attached to mental illness and suicide, I suppose," Anna said.

Chloe wished Anna would look her in the eye. Was there still something she wasn't telling?

"People just can't seem to understand that it's like any other kind of illness," Anna went on. "Some people get cancer, some don't. It's the same with mental illness.

"Before he let me write to you, your father made me promise never to tell you about Roz's illness. I don't feel happy about breaking my promise, but I *can't* let you go on thinking you were to blame for something you can't possibly have done. I — I hope I haven't upset you."

"I wanted to know the truth," Chloe managed. "That's why I came."

Anna looked relieved. "Well, now that you know you aren't to blame, please say you'll stay. I can't tell you how thrilled I was when you said you wanted to visit. I had to re-arrange — well, I mean — I had planned to have someone staying here, but I made other arrangements so you could come."

"Oh," Chloe said. "I'm sorry. I shouldn't have just invited myself like that."

"No, please, don't give it a thought. I wouldn't have mentioned it, only I wanted you to know how much it means to me to see you again after all these years. I couldn't bear to have you leave before we have a chance to get to know one another better. I really want to know what sort of person the little girl I loved has become."

Chloe wavered. She didn't think she could face another encounter with her grandmother like the last one. Yet she felt drawn to Anna. And she owed it to Anna not to leave as quickly and thoughtlessly as she'd arrived. It would be cowardly to turn and run now, before she'd given herself the chance to learn more about her mother. Already she'd found out more here in a day than in ten years with Dad, and Anna would surely tell her more as time went on. There must have been a time when her mother was not ill. What was she like then? And something here might eventually jog her own memory. But still, there was her grandmother. "I could use a night in a proper bed," she said. "That was some bus trip."

Anna nodded. "Good idea. Get a night's sleep and make up your mind in the morning."

"I'd hate to upset Grandma again," Chloe said. "And I don't really mind if she calls me Roz, I guess . . . "

"I'll talk to her doctor and see what he thinks," Anna promised. "These emotional storms are the result of her strokes. After awhile you learn not to take them too personally."

Chloe nodded. Poor Anna. It couldn't be much fun looking after Grandma. No wonder Anna's eyes often looked troubled. Sometimes they almost twinkled, but then, when she thought you weren't looking, they had a kind of haunted expression.

Anna walked to the door. "I'd better go and help her get ready for bed. She's better if nothing upsets her routine."

"Anna," Chloe said as Anna was leaving, "is Gran right? Do I really look like my mother?"

Anna smiled. "I'd have known you anywhere. Goodnight, Chloe. Try to get a good night's sleep."

Left alone, Chloe examined the painting again. The necklace around her mother's neck said Roselinda, but the face wouldn't translate into a proper memory. Maybe, if she hadn't first made the mistake of thinking her mother was Anna, it would have worked. Darn it, anyway.

As she lay in bed her thoughts raced. If my mother had lived, would she look the way Anna looks now? I wonder if I'd have been able to tell the difference between them in real life . . . Chloe flipped over onto her other side as a new thought struck her. If one identical twin was mentally ill, could the other one get it too? Would be rude to ask Anna? And what about kids? Did people inherit mental illness? Each question only seemed to raise half a dozen others.

Chapter Five

Chloe expected to spend a sleepless night. Instead she slept soundly, and late. When she woke, the sunlight was pouring through the two east windows high in the wall above her bed, brightening the pale yellow wallpaper with the tiny blue flowers. It was 9:50 by the bedside clock. The house was silent.

She was in no hurry to get up. Downstairs, she would have to face her grandmother again. She turned on her stomach and glanced up at the painting. It seemed bigger this morning. More overpowering in the small room. The morning light must have something to do with that. She knew the tricks light could play from the observations her art teacher had encouraged her to make. In the painting, Anna had her left hand crossed over her right arm; Roz her right crossed over her left. Mirror-image twins! Funny, she'd never heard of those before. But the portrait itself unlocked no more memories than it had the night before. She gave up and rolled out of bed to go to the bathroom. Outside her door she found a note lying on the floor:

> *Dear Chloe, I've taken Mother to the doctor in Salmon Arm. Decided to let you sleep in. We'll be back about noon. If you go out exploring, please don't go near the cottage next door. It's rented out. Help yourself to breakfast. Love, Anna.*

Good — she wouldn't have to deal with her grandmother straight away. Chloe poured a bowl of cereal and ate it in the breakfast nook, where the window looked out to the lake. The little creaks and groans of the house sounded friendly rather than scary. The house likes me, she thought, even if Grandma Kenyon doesn't.

She decided to take Anna's suggestion — a run, or at least a good walk, would clear her head and help her know whether she should stay or not. And she hadn't been down to the beach yet. Anna's note about the cottage seemed a bit bizarre. Why would Anna think she'd go poking around someone else's cottage? Maybe it just had a deserted look about it, like some rented places did, and Anna was afraid Chloe would assume it was unoccupied?

A short gravelled path ran from the back door to the edge of the lawn, where a log wall held up the bank. A flight of wooden steps led down to the lakeshore. At the top of the steps she stopped to look out over the lake.

It was framed by mountains, not the craggy peaks of the Rockies that she'd travelled through to get here, but rounded. Across the lake a miniature train wound its way around the shoreline and tiny trees and houses dotted the slopes like the scenery for a model railroad. Trucks and cars climbed up a hill, appearing and disappearing in gaps between the trees, the sound of their labouring motors silenced by distance. The silence gave her the feeling of being detached from reality.

Telling herself to snap out of it, she ran down the steps to the beach. A short jetty led over the water to a small building on stilts. She supposed it was the boathouse Anna had mentioned. Sure enough, it housed a boat suspended over the water on a cradle. Its rolled-up sail hung on a wall. Was it the same boat her mother had used when she took her own life? The idea gave Chloe the creeps and she hurried back to the beach.

Grandma Kenyon's property sat on a small bay. To Chloe's left the bay ended where the lake lapped at the foot of the road. To her right it extended about a hundred metres to a rocky outcrop where trees leaned out to the water's edge.

When she'd looked out at it yesterday evening, with the sun on it and a breeze whipping up the surface, the lake had sparkled, full of life. Not today. Under dense grey cloud that had started to move in, the water lay still. Dead. Swallowing her disappointment, Chloe began to walk along the water's edge. The only sound was the crunch of her feet on the pebbles. Everywhere else, an almost eerie silence. The beach was deserted. No birds waded at the water's edge. No children played there. The sky, darker now, hung suffocatingly low. Chloe began to breathe faster. There wasn't enough air and what there was of it clung wet and warm against her face. She tried to brush it away, like you do when you blunder into a spider's web.

The water rippled, licking at Chloe's runners. She edged away, thinking of tides, the water creeping in to trap her against the steep hill . . . Then she pulled herself together. Stupid! — lakes had no tides. But what had caused the sudden movement, then? Nothing. No boats with fanning wakes, no birds alighting or taking off, not even a breeze. At the very edge of the lake the water lapped in short, quick bursts, like an animal panting.

Chloe shuddered. As a child she'd been scared of water. Not just afraid, like some other kids, but terrified. Finally she'd been shamed into swimming lessons by seeing Matthew and Jason take to water like ducks, and now she'd mastered her fear in the swimming pool. But the pool was a manageable size, kept in its place by a rectangular frame of solid wall, its floor hard and predictable. A lake was different. It went its own way, wandering into secret inlets, its depths dark and unknowable.

With a shiver she turned away from the lake and pounded up the pebbly beach. She would climb up to the road and go back that way. The road would probably offer easier walking. But behind the beach tall evergreens, their branches outstretched, crowded down the steep slope, herding her back toward the lake. There was no way up. She'd have to go back the way she had come.

It was a very private bay and the beach lay empty between her and the house. Yet she had the feeling that someone was watching her. A small bungalow stood back from the beach, almost hidden by trees — probably the cottage Anna had told her to stay away from. Preoccupied by the water, she hadn't seen it before when she'd passed. Her aunt had said the cottage was rented, but it appeared to be locked up, the curtains closed and no one home. When she got back the house would be empty too. She felt like the last person on earth, the beach getting narrower and narrower, the water licking in closer and closer to her feet.

Chloe tried to stop the all-too-familiar symptoms. Her heart began to race. She felt dizzy. Sweat soaked her shirt. There was no air. She couldn't breathe.

The panic had her now. She sensed something evil, lurking, unseen, watching her. If she stayed here it would surely kill her. She had to find a place with people. Someone to help her. Maybe there were people on the other side of that rocky outcrop. She remembered seeing cottages when Anna had driven her from the bus.

Legs trembling, she tried to run along the pebbly beach. Her feet slipped on the stones. She was sure she heard someone following her. Not daring to look behind, she forced herself on, but the more she hurried the more the hard edges of the pebbles jabbed through her runners. She ignored the pain.

A flat-bottomed houseboat came into view, progressing steadily down the middle of the lake. Far away the holiday makers sat in chairs on the boat's deck, lost in their own world. Even if she called to them, they wouldn't hear her. Even if she could call.

She didn't think she could. It would be like her nightmare, when she tried to scream for help and was unable to make a sound. Her breath rasped in her throat. Her legs felt too weak to go on. But she had to reach the point of land at the end of the bay. Oh, please God, let there be someone on the other side.

Chapter Six

As Chloe scrambled around the point of land she saw another bay ahead of her, larger than the one she'd escaped. A wooden jetty ran into the water, with a couple of boats anchored close by. More boats had been pulled up on the beach. Nearby, a boy of about her own age stood calmly painting a boat upturned on a stand.

A black pup with a white tip to its tail sniffed about on the beach. As soon as it saw her it galloped up, tail whirling like a toy windmill. She bent and picked it up, hugging its fat, wriggling body against her. Comforted by its puppy smell, Chloe felt her panic gradually subside. She let the pup wipe the salty sweat from her face with its sticky tongue before she put it down.

The boy knelt and whistled to the puppy. He wore a stained T-shirt and cutoffs. His hair was thick and bleached by the sun, his bare arms and legs tanned. "Here, fella," he called. The pup ran over to him.

Chloe made straight for him too. "Hi," she called out, still breathless from her race along the beach. "Is it okay if I sit here for a minute?"

Surprised, he stared at her. "Sure," he said, not sounding sure at all.

Chloe flopped down on the pebbles. In the company of this calm boy, it sounded totally weird to talk about unnamed terrors. She put her fear into more acceptable terms. "I got scared back there. I thought someone was following me."

The boy looked past her, eyes narrowed in concern. Nobody appeared.

"I'll just sit here till I get my breath back," she said. "If that won't bother you."

His colour rose. "No problem," he said, and went on painting his boat.

In a little while Chloe calmed down. "Looks like whoever was following me didn't show up," she admitted, feeling awkward with the boy now that her fear had subsided.

"Maybe thought better of it," he said.

Chloe smiled. That was nice of him. He could've let her know he thought she was stringing him a line. He must be used to girls doing that — he was *so* good looking.

"Funny, I could've sworn there was someone, or something," she said, trying to justify herself. The pup was climbing all over her, biting at her fingers.

The boy gave her a quick look, as though trying to size her up. She waited for him to say something. When he didn't, she rattled on, covering her embarrassment with chatter. "I'm from Edmonton. I'm here on holiday, visiting my aunt and grandmother. I only arrived yesterday. My name's Chloe Griffiths."

His colour deepened. "Danny Wickel," he said. "I live up there." He jerked his head toward the steep slope that rose behind the beach.

Chloe saw a long wooden bungalow perched on a shelf of land. One end of it appeared to be a shop. Over the door hung a sign: WICKELS' MARINA. Groceries • Gas • Fishing licences.

Something clicked in her memory. She hadn't thrown herself on the mercy of a total stranger. "I met your mother yesterday," she said. "She stayed with my grandmother while my aunt went to Salmon Arm to pick me up at the bus station."

He nodded. "Mum does that sometimes. We're neighbours." His tone implied that this was the sort of thing neighbours did.

"Have you lived here long?" Chloe asked, genuinely interested.

"In Salmon Arm my whole life," he said, "but not always right here. When we had the farm, this was just our summer place. The farm's mostly rented out now. We came to live here three years ago — to run the marina."

"So you know my aunt and grandmother pretty well."

"Your aunt was my grade one-teacher in Salmon Arm."

This was a side of Anna's life that Chloe hadn't thought about before. "Really? What was she like? As a teacher, I mean."

For a moment Danny continued his long, slow strokes with the paintbrush, then he paused. "Good, I think. I liked her, anyway." He chuckled, reddening again. "Mum says I didn't want to go into grade two because I wanted to stay with Miss Kenyon."

Chloe smiled. "Your first love affair."

Danny's face reddened. He continued painting with fierce concentration.

Oh no, Chloe thought, now I've embarrassed him. She wanted to keep the conversation going, not only because she was unwilling to face that lonely beach again. She wanted to know more about Danny Wickel. "What's your dog's name?" she asked.

"Buck," he said. "Short for buccaneer."

Chloe smiled. "He does look like a pirate, with that white patch over his eye."

"Push him away if he's bothering you," Danny said.

"Oh, he's not," she said quickly. "I like dogs."

Danny relapsed into silence, concentrating.

He's shy, Chloe thought, really shy, but he doesn't cover it up with talk like I do. His shyness made her feel more comfortable with him. "You must have a good memory," she said, "if you remember how you felt about your grade-one teacher. I don't remember anything about grade one."

He shrugged. "I'm not sure I remember much about Miss Kenyon. As a teacher, I mean. Maybe I just remember the stories my folks tell me. It's kind of hard to know the difference, isn't it?"

"I wouldn't know," Chloe said. "My dad never talks much about the past." The minute she said it she wished she hadn't. Why tell almost a total stranger something like that? She hadn't meant to.

"How come?"

Trying to make it all sound perfectly normal, she said, "I guess it's because my mom died when I was five. She drowned — in this lake, actually. Dad doesn't like to talk about it."

Danny's eyes widened. "Of course. I remember now. Why didn't I clue in? Miss Kenyon had an identical twin, but the sister drowned herself. She must've been your mother." His face flamed again. "Oh, hey, I'm sorry. I didn't mean it to come out like that."

"It's — that's okay," Chloe said. "I don't remember it. Dad married again and I have two half-brothers, Jason and Matthew. Jason's almost seven and Matthew's five. They're not bad little kids. My stepmother's pretty decent, too, but I call her Joyce because — well, you know, I already have a mother, even if she is dead."

As he continued his careful strokes with the paintbrush Danny nodded sympathetically. "Yeah, I guess you could never forget your own mother."

Chloe shifted her position, the stones suddenly uncomfortable. "It's not that simple." Then, seeing him draw back, she softened her tone. "I guess I have a pretty lousy memory," she said, trying to cover up.

He shrugged. "Most people don't remember much from when they were little kids," he said.

"You remember people from when you were five or six."

Concentrating, he frowned. "Not that many." Then he grinned.

She liked his grin.

"I remember this guy," Danny went on. "Stanley Comax. His ears stuck out and he had a face like a monkey. I always liked monkeys. Stan was my best friend . . . But he moved in grade two." He went on with his painting.

"I used to spend my summer holidays here too, until I was about five," Chloe said. "Do you remember me?"

He paused, paintbrush in the air, and thought about it. "I seem to have a vague memory of playing with some other kid when we were here in the summers. Maybe it was you. I remember two of us carrying pails of water from the lake. But I guess, if it was you, you went away and I started school and . . . "

"You met the boy with the monkey face and forgot all about me."

Danny grinned. "Something like that."

Chloe couldn't help liking him. Usually she wasn't very good around boys her own age. They seemed scared of her. Maybe it was her clothes — she wasn't exactly a conventional dresser — but she wasn't going to change her style for anybody. Mostly they weren't interested in the things that interested her, and so she ended up talking a mile a minute — crazy, trivial stuff that must make them think she was an air-head. Yet, here she was, after five minutes, feeling as comfortable with Danny as if she'd known him all her life. "Would it be possible for a five-year-old kid to suffer from amnesia, do you think?"

Again, he thought about it before answering. "Sure, why not? The kid's parents wouldn't notice it, though, would they? I mean a little kid wouldn't have that much to forget."

"I guess not."

Even hinting that she had amnesia about her mother was bad enough. She couldn't let Danny know about her panic attacks. He'd think she was a real freak. "D'you know who rents that cottage next to my grandmother's place?" she asked, changing the subject.

He nodded. "Mrs. Bass. She's an artist — a sculptor. She's been here about a year. She's not home just now. Miss Kenyon said she's gone to Vancouver for a few weeks."

For awhile they were silent. Usually Chloe rushed to fill any lapse in a conversation, but with Danny it somehow didn't seem necessary. Her mind drifted to her grandmother's outburst yesterday, and the fact that she still had to decide whether to stay here or go home.

"My grandmother seems totally out of it," she said. "Yesterday she thought I was my mother."

Danny had finished his painting. He was wrapping his brushes in pieces of plastic. "I wouldn't pay too much attention," he said. "Mum says Mrs. Kenyon used to be a really smart lady; she was a school principal. But when your mother, well, died, it kind of messed up your grandmother. She never really got over it. Mum thinks that's what brought on her first stroke. Now she hardly even remembers who I am, and she's known me nearly all my life."

"Poor Gran," Chloe burst out. "How terrible to be intelligent and then lose it all. It's like this guy I know. He used to be an actor, but then he got cancer and lost his voice. Life can be so cruel."

Danny gazed at her as though he'd found some kind of alien walking along the beach.

Chloe could have bitten out her tongue. Why did she keep blurting out crazy things when she really wanted to get to know Danny? "I guess you think I'm kind of flaky," she said. "Most people do."

"Not really," he said. "I agree, the world's a pretty crazy place." He paused, stowing his brushes in an empty paint can. "My mum might remember your mother. She's got a memory like you wouldn't believe. I'd say, 'like an elephant,' only she'd kill me if she heard."

"Really? That'd be great — if she'd talk to me, I mean, not that she'd kill you."

Danny grinned. Wiping his hands on an oily rag, he said, "If you want to help me carry some of this stuff, you can come up to the house with me. Mum's there. Then, if you like, I'll walk you back to your gran's place along the road. That way you won't have to worry about some creep following you."

It took Chloe a moment to register that. She'd forgotten all about the sense of someone watching her. Even the panic attack had receded from her memory. It was almost as though it had happened to somebody else. She felt happy, like a kid who had just been give a new bike. No, happier even than that. Wow, how could her moods swing like this? Crazy woman, she told herself, but she smiled as she thought it. No one who was really crazy could feel as good as this. Swinging a couple of empty paint cans, she followed Danny up the hill.

Chapter Seven

"We were just going to have a bite of lunch," Marg Wickel said when Chloe and Danny arrived at the house. "If you don't mind pot luck, Chloe, you're welcome to stay."

"That'd be great," Chloe said. Then, hesitating, she added, "But Anna might wonder where I am."

Marg nodded at the phone. "Call her. Number's on the list there."

There was no answer, though. Gran's doctor's appointment must have taken longer than expected, Chloe decided. Well then, why not have lunch with the Wickels? She wouldn't be that long, anyway.

Danny's father came in as Chloe hung up the phone. Paul Wickel was a big man, with strong, square hands. "We do a bit of everything around here," he told her. "We've kept a piece of land closer to town — maybe you noticed the farms as you came through — so we grow some corn. Then we rent out summer cottages and run the marina, and in winter I drive a school bus. You name it, we do it."

Chloe returned his smile. His steady, down-to-earth manner reminded her of Danny.

After they had finished eating, Danny leaned his elbows on the table. "Mum," he said, making the question sound casual, "did you ever meet Chloe's mother?"

Marg looked surprised. "Yes, of course. We were in high school together, Roz and Anna and me."

"You were?" Chloe hadn't expected anything as good as this. It was like being given an unexpected gift. Trying not to sound too eager, she leaned forward. "What was she like when she was young?"

"She was a pretty little thing," Marg said, smiling. "You're very like her."

Chloe wasn't too sure she liked being described as a "pretty little thing." It sure wasn't how she'd describe herself. This threatened to be one of those gifts that let you down when you opened them. "Um — I meant, what was she like as a person? You know."

"Ah," said Marg. "I see. Well, she was lively, intelligent and friendly, and very popular. Every boy in school wanted to date her."

Chloe tried not to look disappointed. Girls who attracted boys like moths around a flame weren't exactly high on her list of favourite people.

"Oh, I don't want to give you the wrong idea," Marg said quickly. "She was popular with us girls too. People were always drawn to her. I suppose she had . . . what do they call it? Charisma, that's it."

44

Something should happen, Chloe thought, somewhere inside me. Some memory should twang like a guitar string.

Danny and his dad were serious now, silently clearing away dishes and making tea, as if trying to give Chloe and Marg their own space.

"I suppose most of us envied Roz a bit," Marg said. "She was the kind of girl who's voted 'most likely to succeed' in the grad yearbook." She smiled, then her expression saddened. "That's why it was so hard to accept — the way her life ended, I mean."

Chloe let the last remark pass. "She doesn't sound much like Anna, even if they were twins," she said.

Marg nodded. "I can see why you'd think that. Anna's so quiet and serious now, but she wasn't always that way. Oh, Roz was the leader, I must admit, but when Anna was young she was full of fun too. They were always joking around, those two. Everyone liked to see them coming. A group might be standing around, griping about life in general, everybody full of doom and gloom, then along would come Roz and Anna and the whole mood of the group would change. Those girls had a real sense of humour. They'd make you see the funny side of things that were getting you down. And they were great mimics." She patted Chloe's arm. "Thank goodness we can't see into the future. It was as if, after Roz died, the sun fell out of Anna's sky."

Mr. Wickel nodded. "She's not been the same since."

"I must ask Anna if she has her school year-book," Chloe said. "She hasn't talked about my mother much. I thought she would. But I suppose we haven't really had much time yet." Especially when you counted the bad scene with Gran.

"Suicide is always hard on the people left behind," Marg said. "It's so easy to blame yourself for something you did, or didn't do. It must be especially hard on Anna — being your mother's twin. They were always so close. She'd be even more inclined to blame herself for not seeing that her sister was in trouble. Anna's had a lot to bear, what with her mother, and all. It's no wonder she's changed."

"She hasn't had an easy time of it," Mr. Wickel added.

"But she doesn't bring her problems to school," Danny said. "She's a popular teacher."

Chloe gave Danny a smile, then turned back to Marg. "I don't remember much about my mother at all," she said. "And nothing about her death."

"Maybe it's kinder that way," Marg said. "I wouldn't be too eager to open old wounds if I were you."

Chloe tensed. Just what did Marg mean by that?

Marg jumped up. "I've just remembered. I've got something you might like to have. I'll be right back."

She came back in a moment carrying a book. "Your mother lent me this. I'd forgotten all about it, but I found it when we were moving here and I was doing some serious throwing out. I offered it to

Anna because it has Roz's name in it. I thought she might like it for a keepsake. But she told me to throw it out. I hadn't the heart, though." She handed the book to Chloe.

"*The Water Babies,* by Charles Kingsley," Chloe read. "It looks like a children's book."

"It is," Marg said.

"I tried to read it once," Danny said. "But I couldn't seem to get into it. I gave up after awhile."

"I remember running into Roz at the doctor's office when you and Danny were babies, Chloe," Marg went on. "Danny's older brother was with me and Roz suggested I read this to him. She said she and Anna had loved the book as children, and that she collected copies. She'd picked this one up at a second-hand bookstore. She wrote her name inside and gave it to me. I thought it was a bit old for Ritchie, so I put it aside to read later, and forgot about it. I guess Roz did, too. You're welcome to keep it if you like."

"Thanks very much, Mrs. Wickel," Chloe said. "I'd love to have it — if you're sure you don't want it. And thanks for lunch." She turned to Danny. "I'd better go. Anna'll be expecting me."

"You could take the eggs with you, if you don't mind," Marg said, suddenly businesslike. "Anna ordered a dozen."

"I'll take them," Danny said. "There was some weirdo following Chloe along the beach this morning. I'll walk her home."

Paul Wickel looked concerned. "Who could that be? Isn't Mrs. Bass away?"

Danny grinned.

Paul Wickel gave him a look. "What's so funny?"

"You fell right into it, Dad. You as good as agreed that Mrs. Bass is weird."

"What's wrong with her?" Chloe asked.

"Nothing," Marg answered, forestalling an argument. "She keeps herself to herself, that's all. She's a sculptor and likes to work in private, Anna says. Doesn't want people watching her work."

Chloe nodded. "I know how she feels. I hate people looking over my shoulder when I paint. Who wants people watching when you make a mess of things?"

"You paint?" Danny asked. "Cool! I need a ruler to draw a straight line."

Marg smiled at Danny. "She comes by it honestly." To Chloe she said, "Your mother was always good at art. I suppose it was one of the interests she and your father had in common."

Chloe blushed. "I'm not that great."

"They say Mrs. Bass is pretty good," Paul Wickel said.

Marg nodded. "She sells her pieces through a Vancouver gallery, except for the soft sculptures. Those go to Salmon Arm for the tourist trade. It's hard to imagine someone who works with stone one minute handling delicate fabrics the next. She must be very talented." She stood up. "I'll go get those eggs ready for you, Chloe. You don't mind waiting a few minutes, do you?"

"No, that's fine."

"Good. And Danny, before you go, could you give

me a hand. I have something heavy that needs moving in the shop." She turned to Chloe. "Will you excuse us? "

"Sure," Chloe said. "I'll look at my mother's book. I don't think I've ever read this — though the pictures seem a little familiar." She began to flip through the book. Its pictures, she decided, were wonderful, full-page illustrations in colour. She wondered if that was why her mother had bought this particular copy. It was nice to think they shared an interest in painting.

As she scanned through the pages there seemed to be something familiar about the story — particularly the characters. Tom . . . The name struck a chord. Of course she might be thinking of something else. There must be dozens of Toms in children's books.

Then she stopped at a picture of a strange character called Mrs. Doasyouwouldbedoneby. The picture was as weird as the name. It showed an old-fashioned kind of granny wearing reading glasses. Obviously the illustration was supposed to appeal to a child, but Chloe found it just the opposite. There was something threatening about it. She skimmed some of the pages. The more she read, the more familiar the story felt, and yet it wasn't a comfortable feeling. There was something about the book that made her feel vaguely uneasy. When Danny came back and asked if she was ready to go, she closed the book and jumped up, happy to put it out of her mind.

As they walked along the road to Gran's house

Danny asked, "Did Mum tell you anything useful?"

"Sure," she said, not wanting to sound ungrateful. "It all adds to the picture. You know, bit by bit." What had she been expecting when she'd decided to come here? A flash of light, maybe, a sort of "Wow! I remember my mother!" She was beginning to see that nothing like that was going to happen. It would be more like putting a jigsaw puzzle together, one piece at a time. If the *Water Babies* book was a piece of the puzzle, a clue to her mother's personality, she had no idea where it fitted.

"This is where your Gran's property starts," Danny said, nodding at a telephone pole beside the road. "Most people around here don't own much more than a strip of land between the road and the lake. Mrs. Kenyon's property is a lot wider than most, except ours, but ours is steeper. Mrs. Bass's cottage is just below us, but you can't see it because of the trees."

"Why don't you like her?" Chloe asked.

He shrugged. "It's not a matter of not liking her. I hardly know her. She's kind of creepy, that's all. Never mixes with the neighbours. Never invites anyone in. I wouldn't mind betting it was her following you this morning. She's like that. Can't stand anyone near her place. The only one she gets along with is Miss Kenyon. Once in a while you see them in Salmon Arm doing a bit of shopping together, or taking in a movie, or something, but that's about it."

The artist, Chloe thought, needing her own

space to work in. She could understand that, even sense why Danny didn't. "I thought you said she'd gone away."

"Yeah," he admitted grudgingly. "But I wouldn't put it past her to sneak back."

Chloe changed the subject since Danny obviously wasn't going to change his mind about Mrs. Bass. "Is Salmon Arm a big place? I didn't get to see very much of it. Anna brought me straight here from the bus."

He rolled his eyes. "It's not exactly New York, but if you'd like to take a look around, we could go in the boat. It's faster than by road. I want to give the boat another coat of paint, and then let it harden before I put it back in the water, but it should be okay by the weekend."

Danny's offer took Chloe completely by surprise. Did he think she'd been angling for a date? "Thanks," she said. That didn't sound very enthusiastic, and she *did* want to go with him, so she added, "I'd like that." Then she was afraid she sounded like she was coming on too strong. "I mean, it'd be fun to go by boat. And thanks for letting me talk to your mum, and for walking me home."

"No problem," Danny said, handing her the eggs. "See ya."

His grin drove everything else out of her mind. He likes me, she thought. Smiling, she floated down the path and in by the back door.

Anna was in the kitchen.

"Hello, Chloe," she said, taking the bag of eggs

out of Chloe's arms. "I guess you've met Danny Wickel, if you're delivering my eggs." She smiled. "How do you feel today?"

"Fine," said Chloe. Terrific, she thought. I feel like climbing a mountain, or skimming across the lake on one of those sailboards. What's got into me?

"Then you've decided to stay awhile?"

Had there ever been any doubt about it? "Yes," she said. "That is, if it's still okay." She could see by Anna's smile that it was.

Anna removed the eggs from the bag, then pulled out the book Marg had given Chloe. She stared at it for a moment, her smile fading. "Where did you get this?"

"Mrs. Wickel gave it to me," Chloe said, surprised by Anna's reaction. "My mother lent it to her and she forgot to return it. See, my mother wrote her name on the flyleaf. Danny's mum thought I might like it for a keepsake."

Anna frowned slightly. "A keepsake? Oh, I don't think so, Chloe. It isn't a particularly pleasant book."

"But — but Danny's mum said my mother told her it was a favourite of hers and yours when you were children," Chloe said, puzzled.

"Roz's favourite, maybe, but not mine."

"I haven't really read it yet," Chloe said. "I mainly looked at the pictures. I didn't really like the one of that creepy woman." She ran her hand over the well-worn cover. "But I don't have anything else that belonged to my mother."

"I'm sorry, Chloe," Anna said, looking stricken.

"I've been thoughtless. Would you like to have your mother's necklace? The one she was wearing in the portrait — the one with her name on it? It's in a drawer somewhere. I'll find it for you."

"Thanks," Chloe said. "I *would* like it — very much." She hesitated. "But I think I'd still like to keep the book."

"Well, that's up to you, of course," Anna said. "I'll go and look for that necklace now, before I forget."

Curious to see what Anna didn't like about the book, Chloe read rapidly while she was gone. The story was about a poor little Victorian chimney sweep called Tom, who drowned in a river. A sort of fairy godmother, Mrs. Doasyouwouldbedoneby, watched over him. Her name pretty well said it all. Tom was supposed to become a water baby, but at first he couldn't find the others, so he had to make do with creatures like dragonflies, lobsters and caddises for company. Chloe frowned. What on earth was a caddis? And what did a dragonfly look like before it turned into a dragonfly? Judging by the description, it sounded gross.

On the whole, she had to agree with Anna — the story wasn't very appealing. But maybe her mother had been fascinated by insects. Some kids were. Jason, for instance. He had quite a collection of plastic ones that he knew all about. Her tastes ran more to animals with four legs, cuddly things like teddy bears and rabbits. Anna must feel more the way she did.

For the time being she went to her room and hid the book under the clothes in her drawer, so that

Anna wouldn't see it and be upset. Then she ran back downstairs and was almost in the kitchen when the phone rang. It seemed to startle Anna, who jumped to answer it.

"For you," she said, sounding surprised. "It's Danny Wickel."

Chloe took the receiver.

"Hi," Danny said. "Stinking hot, isn't it?"

"Yes," Chloe agreed. The sky was still grey, but the day was hot. Humid too. Now that he mentioned it, she felt sticky.

"I thought I'd go for a swim," he said. "To cool off. Want to come?"

"Okay," she said, hoping he meant at some pool. "Where?"

"Off the end of our jetty."

Her heart sank. But it was too late to back out now.

"I'll pick you up in my truck," he went on. "It's too hot to walk back over from your place again. I can be there in five minutes."

"Can you make it in about an hour?" Chloe asked. "I haven't been able to spend much time with Gran or Anna yet."

"Don't worry about us, Chloe," Anna said. "We can visit later. Now that you've decided to stay for a week or two, we'll have lots of time to talk."

Chloe smiled her thanks and turned back to the phone. "Anna says it's fine. See you in five?"

When Chloe hung up, Anna held out her hand. "By the way, I found your mother's necklace." She handed it to Chloe.

"Thanks, Anna. This is really special." She wanted to put it on right away, but decided that would be taking a chance when she was going to be swimming. She'd hate to lose it in the water. "I'll put it up with my things," she told Anna, and ran upstairs to her bedroom.

By the time Chloe had tucked the necklace into her drawer, changed into a bathing suit and borrowed a towel from Anna, Danny's truck announced his arrival with squeaking brakes.

"I have to do something about that," he said, wincing.

"I'm not the best swimmer in the world," Chloe admitted as she climbed up into the cab of Danny's beat-up old Ford. "Actually, I'm a bit of a chicken in the water."

"Don't worry," he said. "The lake stays shallow for a long way out. You can't get into trouble. Anyway, I'll be there. The bottom's a bit soft underfoot for the first few metres. That's why we use the jetty. You can swim without wading out."

Soft. Did he mean slimy, the sort of stuff that sucked your feet in? She hoped she wouldn't make a fool of herself. If she had a panic attack right in front of Danny . . . The idea alone was enough to make her palms sweat.

They rattled along the narrow, bumpy road with the truck windows open to catch a breeze. The noise made it almost impossible to talk, so Chloe used the time to lecture herself on not freaking out in the water. After a short ride they parked the truck above Danny's place and walked downhill to the lake.

Danny dived in and Chloe forced herself to slide off the jetty. After the first, small shock, the water felt warm and the lake was glassy smooth, calmer even than a swimming pool, and not very deep. What she mostly hated was having water cover her face when she wasn't expecting it. This was okay. She settled into her crawl and followed Danny.

"I thought you said you couldn't swim," Danny teased. "Race you to that boat."

Chloe started off toward where Danny had pointed. Of course, it was no contest. But at least she'd proved she wasn't a total wimp. A reward for all those hours of suffering through swimming lessons. They held onto the side of the boat and bobbed while they talked, Chloe conscious of the water, silkily cool, sliding over her skin, and Danny close by, almost close enough to touch.

"We could, um, maybe go to Salmon Arm on Saturday," Danny said, not looking at her. "The second coat of paint on the boat will be hardened by then. If you want to come along for the ride, we could take in a movie maybe."

"Sure," she said, trying to sound casual. "That'd be great." She pushed herself off with her legs. "Race you back to shore."

Chapter Eight

In return for the swim, Chloe offered to help Danny work on his boat the following day. It was hot, hard work, and much as she liked being with Danny, she felt a bit guilty for spending so much time with him rather than with Gran and Anna, so left him to do the sanding while she headed back to Anna's. By the time she got back, Anna was in the kitchen making tea and a snack for Grandma Kenyon.

"Danny's a nice boy, isn't he?" Anna asked.

"Mmm." Chloe nodded while she ate one of Anna's cookies. The mention of Danny reminded her that she should probably get Anna's permission before she went to Salmon Arm with him. "Is it okay if I go to Salmon Arm with Danny on Saturday?" she asked. Anna seemed to be off somewhere else, as if she had to collect her thoughts before she could answer.

"I don't see why not," she finally said. "Is he driving?"

"No. We're taking the boat. You know, the one

he's been painting. He's overhauled the engine, too. He wants to give it a real tryout."

"That sounds like Danny. He's crazy about boats. You won't forget to wear your life jacket, will you? I'm sorry to sound like a fuss-budget, but . . . " She broke off and gave Chloe a quick, apologetic smile. "Oh well, no doubt you're used to being fussed over."

"Not by Joyce," Chloe said.

The kettle boiled, venting steam into the kitchen. Anna lifted it from the stove as it began its piercing whistle. "I suppose she's too busy with her own little boys."

Over the sound of water pouring into the pot, Chloe heard Anna's tone of disapproval. "No, Joyce doesn't fuss over the boys either. Like when Jason wants to go out without a jacket she says, 'Go outside and see how cold it is and then decide.' If he thinks he doesn't need it, she lets him go. She says he only needs to get cold once and he'll learn."

"Considering Edmonton winters, that's taking a bit of a risk, isn't it?"

Inside, Chloe sighed. She'd given Anna the wrong idea. Now she felt disloyal to Joyce. "Not really. It saves a lot of fights. Anyway, Joyce doesn't try to mother me and I like it that way."

Anna turned, her expression stricken. "I'm sorry, Chloe. I didn't realize . . . "

"Oh — Anna — it's okay. I didn't mean you, you're different. Being around you is . . . well, it's almost like being around my own mother, isn't it? Somehow, I don't mind it when you fuss over me."

Anna's cheeks flushed. "Thank you. I take that as a compliment," she said. Her wide smile made her eyes crinkle at the corners.

Chloe smiled back. Was this more like the old Anna that Marg Wickel had tried to describe?

"And since you don't mind my fussing," Anna added with a smile, "while you're in town I want you to pick up some more sunscreen lotion. Your arm looks a bit red between the freckles. We redheads have to be careful."

It was the first time Anna had tried to joke a little. Chloe felt it marked a step forward in their relationship. Usually Anna seemed too unsure of herself, as if she was afraid to say the wrong thing.

"I'm glad you and Danny get along so well," Anna went on. "I was afraid you'd be bored here."

Talking about Danny, Chloe decided, was the next best thing to being with him. Besides, she felt a sudden urge to share confidences with Anna. "Did you know Danny was in love with you in grade one?"

"Hmph. He wouldn't be the first boy to fall in love with his grade-one teacher," Anna said. Smiling, she bent over a bread board, cutting a small brown loaf into thin slices for Grandma Kenyon. "They feel quite differently about you when they get to grade eight, believe me."

Was Anna happy, Chloe wondered, teaching school and looking after Gran? It must be a pretty boring life. Had she ever married? Ever been in love?

Before Chloe could ask, Anna handed her a tray.

"Take this through to Mother, please, and I'll bring in the teapot. And Chloe, if she calls you Roz, just play along, like we decided, will you? Dr. Como agreed it would help keep your grandmother less confused."

Chloe nodded and carried the tray into the living room. Gran looked up and smiled. As Anna had forecast, Gran had totally forgotten her anger of the first day. But still, she wasn't like the grandmotherly woman on the bus, and Chloe was still a bit wary of her moods.

"Thank you, dear," Grandma Kenyon said as Chloe put the tray on the coffee table. "Come here and sit beside me." She pointed with her cane to a footstool near her feet. "We haven't seen much of each other lately. What have you been doing with yourself?"

"Mostly helping Danny around the marina," Chloe said.

"Danny? Who's Danny?"

"Marg Wickel's son. A tall blond guy. Sometimes he delivers eggs here. You know him."

"No, I can't say I do. He's a summer visitor, I suppose." Grandma Kenyon looked fondly at Chloe and shook her head. "Your daddy doesn't approve of all these boyfriends you collect. But I must admit I'm glad to hear about this new one. He might take your mind off Owen."

Owen! Her father. A tingle, like a small electric shock, ran through her.

"Owen's not for you, Roz darling," Gran went on. "Oh, I know you think you love him, but there'll be someone else. People are drawn to you, my golden girl, and someone else will come along to make you happy. Perhaps this new boy you seem so taken with. But Owen's the only one Anna will ever love. Let him go, Roz. Let him go to Anna."

Chloe bent closer. What was Gran saying — that both her mother and Anna had loved her father? She wanted to ask Gran what she meant, but . . .

"Chloe," Anna called from the hall. "Would you open the door? My hands are full."

Chloe sighed. After that, Gran's mind was more on her tea, the past forgotten, at least for now.

But Chloe couldn't put Grandma Kenyon's remarks out of her mind. She felt guilty, as if she'd been spying on Anna and found out something she shouldn't know. If Gran was right, Anna had loved Dad, but he had married her twin sister. Anna would be mortified if she knew Chloe knew about it. It was like trespassing on Anna's privacy, but still she couldn't help thinking about it. No wonder Dad had never wanted to come back here. Even after Roz died, he hadn't wanted to marry Anna. Poor Anna! Chloe felt like such a hypocrite, pretending not to know.

At breakfast the next morning she tried to put things right. Gran was having her breakfast in bed, so Chloe and Anna were alone. Given a chance, Anna might tell what had happened when she and Roz and Chloe's dad were young. They could get everything out in the open. It had been so long ago, anyway, they would probably laugh about it.

"Anna, since you and my mother were so alike, did you ever like the same boy?" She could feel her cheeks turn pink. "It'd be natural, wouldn't it, being twins?"

"People always ask twins that," Anna said. "They never stop to think that the third party might have some say in the matter. You can't just divide up the spoils, you know. But I suppose you're mainly thinking of your father, are you? Well, it's true that when we first knew him, Roz and I both found him attractive, but it was Roz he fell in love with and I accepted that. It wasn't a problem."

"But Gran said . . . " Chloe stopped, blushing. She hadn't meant to betray Gran, but now she'd gone this far she had to carry on. "It wasn't Gran's fault, honestly, but you know how she always thinks I'm my mother, so she said something that made me think my mother, well, kind of stole him — Dad, I mean — from you. I mean, girls do that sometimes, don't they?"

"Not Roz and I. She and I never fought over a man in our lives. Unfortunately, not even Mother totally understood us. She thought Roz dominated me." Anna sighed. "If that were true — and I really don't think it was — I didn't mind at all. Whatever made Roz happy, made me happy, and that included her happiness with the man she loved. Owen."

She jumped up and started to clear the table. "By the way, I'm taking your grandmother to have lunch with some old friends. I can give you a ride to Wickels' place. If you'd like to take a picnic, feel free to raid the fridge." And she was gone before Chloe even had time to answer.

Chloe stared at the doorway Anna had just gone through. Was it true that Anna and Roz had never fought over a boyfriend? Chloe couldn't imagine a girl giving up a guy she loved, even for her twin sister. Well, true or not, Anna had just put a lid on this conversation. Chloe sighed. Dad and Anna might not like one another, but they sure had one thing in common — their determination to keep secrets.

Chapter Nine

When Anna dropped Chloe off, Danny's boat was already in the water. White paint sparkling, it bobbed at the end of the jetty, rising on the wake of a motorboat that was zooming out of sight. It looked almost posed for a photograph, Chloe thought, the kind you see on a travel poster, all sunshine and blue rippling water against a background of purple hills. And Danny in the foreground, blond, tanned and looking sensational, was as good as a poster too. Better, because he was here in the flesh.

Dangling her legs over the side of the jetty, she spread sunscreen on her arms. "How come you don't need this stuff?" she asked him. "You're so blond you shouldn't be able to get such an amazing tan."

And your eyes are subtle, she thought, trying not to look like she was looking at him. They'd be difficult to paint. On a sunny day, like today, they looked blue, and when it was cloudy they turned grey. They reflected the sky, or maybe, like today, the lake . . .

"I'm outside a lot all year round." Danny shrugged. "My skin's just tougher, I guess."

Chloe smiled. Most good-looking boys thought they were so hot, but Danny didn't seem like that at all.

He glanced at the sky. "The sun's fierce today. Got a hat?"

"Anna lent me one of hers, but it makes me feel like Scarlett O'Hara." She pulled it out of her bag and set it on her head.

"It's okay. But it might blow off."

"Then how about this?" She produced a wide green visor from her beach bag. "Anna says they were 'all the rage' a few years ago." She put it on. "I think I look like one of those newspaper men in old movies."

Danny grinned. "It doesn't do much for the back of your neck. Here, wear this." He pulled a towel from his duffel bag and tossed it to her.

"Like a shawl?" She draped it around her shoulders.

"No, like this." He threw it over her head. "Let it dangle down behind. You can use the visor to anchor it. Here, I'll hold the towel while you put the visor on."

His hand was warm and carried a faint scent of soap. She wanted to hold it next to her cheek and close her eyes and absorb the way his skin smelled . . . Better cool down, she thought, remembering the kids at school — the breaking up, the getting back together again, the giggles, the fights, the gossip, the comments. This was different. She didn't want to spoil it.

She wondered if he'd sensed what she was feeling, but already he was bent over the boat again, fiddling with something. Slowly she pulled on her life jacket and fumbled with the fastening. "No wonder people don't want to wear these things," she said. "They're so hot and clumsy."

He looked up. "They used to be a lot worse. Haven't you ever worn one before?"

"Only in the pool," she said. "We had to practise falling out of a canoe."

"You never went to a lake with your dad?"

"No. Dad says the lakes in Alberta are nothing but sloughs."

Danny didn't ask why her dad had never brought her here, to see Gran and Anna. Maybe he was being tactful. Maybe he already knew why — from his mother, something about Anna having loved Owen. Maybe even about the mental illness her mother had suffered . . . What else might he know that he hadn't told her?

Danny grabbed the side of the boat and held it against the jetty. "Hop in." Buck beat Chloe to it. Danny laughed and lifted the puppy out. "Not you, Buck. You have to stay home. Here you go, Chloe, aim for the middle and sit down right away. Then you won't get dunked."

Once clear of the jetty, Danny gunned the boat forward. "Pretty cool, eh?" he yelled over the noise of the motor, proud of its performance.

"Right!" she yelled back, smiling, proud of his skill. The boat bounced over the surface. Chloe let herself enjoy the ride. It was useless to talk over the roar of the motor and the *smack, smack* of the hull on the water.

"Hang on." Danny pushed the engine to full power. From under the boat's bows the water raced back at dizzying speed. The wind snatched the breath out of Chloe's mouth. It was like flying.

Then the engine choked and sputtered to a stop. In the silence Danny's voice seemed to come from far away, deadened, as if her ears were plugged after a plane flight.

"I don't get it. It was going great. Hang on, Chloe, I'll get it fixed."

The boat drifted lifelessly on the bright, rippling water. The shore seemed far away. The ripples made Chloe slightly dizzy. She wanted to look away, but couldn't. Below the surface the light shimmered, reminding her of heat waves rising over an Alberta road in midsummer. She thought she glimpsed something white floating under the surface. She wanted to call out to Danny, but her tongue felt stuck to the roof of her mouth. Slight waves from a passing boat stirred the water and the image slid out of symmetry, like a rock with a fault.

All at once she was terrified. She squeezed her eyes shut. Even if she couldn't see them, there were other things under the water, she knew it — things like the ones she saw in her nightmares. Horrible things. Grotesque fish. Strange crustaceans with bulging eyes and waving antennae, feeling, exploring, climbing over each other. Things with pale tentacles — bloodless, boneless, wet and cold and white as death, waiting to drag her down. She couldn't breathe. She had to get away.

She leaped up, clambered over the back seat, scrambled to Danny and grabbed his arm. The boat rocked sickeningly.

"What are you doing!"

Danny used a curse that shocked Chloe back to her senses. She collapsed onto a seat. She turned around and sat with her back to him. There was nothing in the water . . . Nothing at all . . . In spite of the sun blazing from the noonday sky, she was covered in goosebumps.

Danny got the engine started again and slowly accelerated. He said nothing to Chloe, and then the roar of the motor was the only sound.

As the boat headed for the marina at Salmon Arm, Chloe's heart gradually stopped pounding. Beside the boat millions of tiny bubbles, each filled with light, tumbled and bounced. The wake made waves like mirrors angled to the sun. Across the lake the mountains were dark blue. Chloe hugged her hands between her knees. I'm *not* crazy, she thought. I'm not. Those horrible things she had imagined, the creatures of her nightmare — she knew now where they came from.

"Look for a place to tie up," Danny called to her as they drew into the marina. But he found one himself when Chloe didn't reply.

She waited while he brought the boat in beside

the jetty and killed the motor. He jumped ashore and tied up, then held the boat steady while she passed up their bags and scrambled out. Through it all she avoided looking at him.

Silent, he led the way along the jetty and up a steep ramp. He didn't stop when they reached the pier, but kept going. The pier was a long one, bare and hot. Chloe struggled to keep up. When they reached the park at the end of the pier Danny dropped his bag on a picnic bench and threw himself down on the grass beside it.

Head down, her arms hugging her drawn-up knees, Chloe huddled a few metres away where a young tree offered a small patch of shade. What must he think of her? "I'm sorry — " she began.

At the same time he said, "Look, I'm sorry."

She stared at him. *"You're* sorry? What for?"

"For swearing at you like that." His face flamed. "You scared me, jumping around in the boat like that, but I shouldn't have — "

"It was my own fault," she said. "It was a really dumb thing to do."

"Why did you?"

He was looking at her as though he thought she must have some reason for acting like a total idiot. She had to tell him something. Not telling would make her look worse. Maybe if she explained about her nightmare. Lots of people had nightmares. They discussed them over cans of pop, trying to find out what the dreams meant.

"Okay," Chloe began. "this is what I think happened. I must have fallen asleep — just for a second or two. Time plays tricks when you sleep. You know, you think you've been dreaming for ages and it's really only a few seconds? Anyway, it was warm and the boat was rocking — and — and I had this nightmare I sometimes get."

He nodded, giving her his full attention.

"This nightmare — it's totally bizarre. Grotesque. There's this body in the water. I can see it — all distorted by the light. I know if I reach out to help, I'll fall in. And there are these creepy things under the water, waiting to drag me down."

"Creepy things?"

"Remember that book your mother gave me? *The Water Babies?*"

"Yes, that story I didn't finish reading."

"Well, I've read it. At least, I think my mother must have read it to me when I was little. It has these descriptions of insects in it. I've always hated things with more than four legs, especially if they wave those creepy antennae in front of them."

Danny nodded. "Horror movie stuff."

"And nightmares." Danny was making her feelings about creepy-crawly things seem normal. "I bet they freaked me out when I was little and I shoved them to the back of my mind, but they wriggled into my nightmare, because you have no control over dreams, do you?"

Again he nodded, encouraging her to go on.

The only thing was, she couldn't explain about the body. She didn't tell him she knew the body was her drowning mother, or how she woke up from the nightmare sweating, shaking with fear, knowing she was no good, not normal . . . She'd spent hours and hours trying to interpret her own dream. All she could come up with was that she'd done something terrible — something to do with her mother, maybe somehow caused her death. But, according to Anna, that was impossible. So what *was* the nightmare really about?

"There was this little girl in the story," Chloe went on. "Ellie. She drowned too, later, and became Tom's friend. Maybe there's some sort of connection there."

Danny gazed over the shallows to where a heron patiently fished. At last he leaned forward, serious. "My guess is that something scary happened to you when you were a little kid. It's part of what you can't remember. Maybe you almost drowned, or thought you were drowning, or something. That's why you're so scared of water. And then your mother . . . well . . . drowned, and your brain tried to put the pieces together while you were asleep, and gave you a nightmare."

Nightmare was right. All those grotesque animals! Was she developing some mental illness, like her mother? She couldn't tell Danny about *that*. She either had to make a joke of it, or burst into tears. "How d'you feel about having a crazy person for a friend?" she asked.

"We-ell, we're all a bit crazy, aren't we? I know I am."

"You? That's the dumbest thing I ever heard."

The blood rushed to Danny's face. "What makes you say that? You hardly even know me."

"Okay, so tell me. How are you crazy?"

"I have this thing," he said finally. "About girls. They scare the life out of me."

"But you're not scared of me."

"No. Not of you." Danny looked down, his eyes shaded by his thick eyelashes. "You're the first girl I've ever liked." He gave her a shy grin. "See, you and I are alike. Two crazies."

Chloe smiled. He likes me, she thought. I don't believe it.

His grin widened. "So what do you want to do first? Eat lunch, or see the sights?"

"What about you?"

"Eat. I'm starving."

This has to be one of the happiest moments of my life, and all he wants to do is eat, Chloe thought. But she didn't feel angry. To her surprise she felt warm and tender. She reached for her beach bag. "Then you're in luck, 'cause guess what! Anna suggested I bring a picnic."

Danny pointed to his duffel bag. "Mum sent along what she calls 'a little snack.' Luckily, I could eat a horse."

After they had eaten lunch he pulled her to her feet and kept her hand in his as they set off for town.

What's happening to me? Chloe wondered. Only an hour ago I thought I'd totally lost it. Now I feel so normal I can't believe it. She smiled at the people they passed, tourists some of them. Little kids sucking popsicles. Middle-aged ladies licking ice-cream cones. Men in ridiculous shorts and eye-shocking shirts and silly caps, proudly bearing fishing rods. People smiled back, or gazed at her wonderingly. They can see, she thought. They can see how happy I am.

Chapter Ten

After their visit to Salmon Arm, Chloe saw Danny almost every day. His invitations were usually just casual.

"You should see Margaret Falls," he said. "It's our local tourist attraction. I'll give you a ride over there."

"You've never been fishing? You haven't lived." And he took her to his favourite fishing spot.

Chloe didn't care much for fishing, but she liked to sit beside the clear running water with her sketch pad on her knee. Before another week had gone by, she had sketches of Danny fishing, Danny working on a boat engine, Danny diving off the marina jetty, Danny building a campfire. They were not portraits, just studies in action, but she tinted one with her pastels and gave it to his parents because they obviously loved it.

She hadn't forgotten her plan to do a portrait of Gran, either. Gran seemed to enjoy sitting quietly in her favourite armchair, or outside on a deck chair, while Chloe sketched nearby.

One morning Chloe was sitting at the kitchen table, trying to work up one of her sketches of Gran, while Anna fussed about in the kitchen. As far as Chloe could tell, she was not accomplishing very much. Occasionally she glanced at Chloe, looking as though she wanted to ask her something.

"Is something wrong?" Chloe asked.

Anna took a deep breath. "I was wondering if you'd — " she began, but broke off. "No, it's probably not a good idea."

"What isn't?" Chloe asked.

"Well, I'd like to go out tomorrow evening and I thought — I was wondering, if you would mind staying home with your grandma. Only . . . "

"Sure. I'd be glad to." Helping with Gran was one way Chloe could repay Anna for having her to visit.

Anna still looked doubtful. "Your grandma can be a bit difficult at times."

"You don't have to worry. Gran and I get along really well these days and I'm used to baby-sitting the boys. Gran can't be harder to mind than those two."

"It would save asking Marg Wickel. I know she's busy at this time of year. I could leave a telephone number where you could reach me."

What's the matter with her, doesn't she think I can handle the job? Chloe wondered. I've been here nearly two weeks already.

"I'm glad you're not letting your grandmother's moods get to you, Chloe," Anna went on. "You can't pay too much attention to the things she says, you know. She can get some pretty far-out ideas some-times."

So *that* was what was worrying Anna. More revelations from Gran about Anna's past — like the one about her being in love with Dad. What other skeletons were hiding in the family closet? A thought occurred to her. "Anna, who stays with Gran when you're at school?" she asked. "Mrs. Bass?"

Anna looked startled. "What do you know about Mrs. Bass?" she asked.

"Nothing much. Danny said she rents your cottage. He said she's a sculptor, but that she's away right now." She was sorry she'd brought the matter up. She was making Danny sound like a gossip.

"I see. Well, he's right about Mrs. Bass being away, but even when she's here she doesn't stay with Mother. She's too busy with her work. Mother has a good friend in Salmon Arm. I drop her off there on my way to school and her friend takes her to the Seniors' Centre. They play cards and do crafts. The company's good for her. Now, you're sure you don't mind about staying with her?"

"I'm sure Gran and I will be okay. Where are you going tomorrow? Got a date?"

Again Anna looked startled. "I've known Dr. Como for so long it's hard to think of him as a date."

"And who's this Dr. Como?"

"My doctor. Well, not really mine. Mother's. He's a widower."

"Where's this guy taking you?"

"To the fanciest restaurant in town." At last,

Anna smiled. "Enjoy your casserole while I'm dining on lobster."

Thinking maybe she could help Anna's love life along, Chloe asked, "Tomorrow, can I do your hair? I love doing hair."

"Oh, no, thank you, Chloe. I don't think so. I always wear it this way."

"I won't cut it, or anything," Chloe promised. "Don't worry, I won't do anything outrageous."

After Chloe had finished with it the next evening, Anna's red hair framed her face in a casual, wind-blown style. Chloe stood back to have a better look. Yes, released from its knot and smoothed with Chloe's curling iron, Anna's hair looked much better. Chloe was about to say, "You look ten years younger," before she decided it sounded rude. "You look gorgeous," she said instead.

Grandma Kenyon was as pleased as Chloe with the transformation. "How lovely you look, my darling Anna," she said. Blushing, Anna bent to kiss her good-bye. Gran took Anna's face between her hands. "You've always been beautiful, Anna dear. Such a pity that you let yourself live under a shadow."

That's it exactly, Chloe thought. She's like a birch tree in the fall. When the sky's cloudy the leaves are quite an ordinary yellow, but in the sunlight they shine like gold. Except the sun never shines on Anna. It's as if she's waiting for the clouds to pass.

The doorbell rang and Anna whisked into the

hall, closing the door behind her. Chloe was surprised by Anna's quick exit. Oh well, I guess I'll get to meet the good doctor some other time, Chloe thought. She can't keep him under wraps forever. Dutifully she put Anna and her date out of her mind, and turned her attention to her grandmother. "What would you like to do, Gran?" she asked. "Watch TV?"

Grandma Kenyon shook her head. "There's nothing I care to see."

Anna had said it was important to keep Gran's mind occupied, almost like doing brain exercises. Chloe went over the possibilities. A board game? Possibly. Gran really preferred cards but Chloe was no good at them. A jigsaw puzzle? No, they'd just finished one.

Inspiration! A photo album. Anna had let her borrow a few. Maybe Gran might enjoy remembering the old times. She'd said herself that she remembered the past better than the present.

"I'll be right back," Chloe said, and dashed up to her room to get an album. On an impulse, she decided to put on her mother's necklace. She lifted it from the drawer and fastened the clasp, admiring how pretty it looked lying against her black T-shirt. Downstairs again, she pulled up a stool beside her grandmother's chair and opened the album on Gran's lap. "Look what I found," she said.

"Why, that's Daddy." Gran smiled. "He was such a handsome man. That's where you and Anna get your good looks, my dear." She leaned forward to take a closer look. "Of course he was much younger then. We'd just built this house. You can see it hasn't been stained yet and the new wing isn't built." Chuckling, she pointed to another snapshot. "There's that little dog we used to have. Giggles you called it. Silly name for a dog."

What a weird thing memory was, Chloe thought. Gran could remember a dog's name from years ago, but not what she'd had for dinner.

"And this is you and Anna learning to swim. Daddy taught you." Gran smiled. "That's you, the one splashing about like a fish. There's Anna, shivering. She never took to the water the way you did. You're like Daddy. He was a wonderful swimmer. When he was young he played water polo. Did you know that? And he loved to sail." Her eyes misted over. "He'd be so proud of his little Roz for winning those yacht races out at the coast."

A thought stuck in Chloe's mind. If her mother had been such a good sailor and swimmer, how had she managed to drown herself? She must have made sure she couldn't change her mind at the last minute. And how would she have done that? Maybe weighted herself down with a rock . . . Maybe that's why they never found her body . . . Chloe shuddered and thrust the image out of her mind. "I can never tell who's who in these pictures," she said. "Could you? In real life, I mean."

"Oh, usually. At least, when you were together." Gran gazed at the snapshot, her memories softening her face, making her voice gentle.

Chloe glanced up. There were times when Gran was so lovable and loving that it was easy to forget how unkind she'd been at first. Hard to believe, right now, that Gran's moods were hard to predict, and that without warning she could turn sharp and waspish.

"When you were children you used to want to wear the same clothes," Gran went on, "so I insisted on different colours. That way we could tell at a glance who was who. As you got older you chose different clothes, but you were always borrowing from one another. So Daddy bought you necklaces with your names designed in gold. Why, you're wearing yours now. I hadn't noticed before."

Chloe felt hot. She'd been thoughtless. The necklace might have upset Gran. "But — with one liking the water and one not, that's not exactly alike, is it?" she asked, trying to turn Gran's attention away from the necklace.

"No, not exactly," Gran said. "You were the leader. Anna was quieter, but you were both impetuous. 'Girls, think before you act,' Daddy would say. But it was no good. You were like those animals you see on nature shows. What do you call them? They have horns. You see a baby leap into space. You hold your breath, but it lands with all four feet on some jagged bit of rock."

"Mountain goats," said Chloe.

Gran didn't pay any attention. Lost in her own reminiscences, she seemed to have forgotten Chloe. "You would always land on your feet," she went on. "Anna would sometimes slip and fall, but you were always there to pick her up and dust her off. Anna was the one I worried about. You were the sure-footed one. Until . . . " Her face began to crumple and tears welled up in her eyes.

Chloe tried to close the book. "Let's do something else now," she said.

With a start, Grandma Kenyon came back to the present. She stared at Chloe and gripped the album so that Chloe couldn't take it away. "No. There's something wrong," she said. "Let me think. That was Anna who went out just now."

"Yes, Gran."

"Why do you keep calling me Gran?"

"I . . . I don't know. I'm sorry." Chloe felt nervous. She'd slipped up, and now she was losing control of the situation.

"Yes, you do know," Grandma Kenyon said, in one of her sudden bursts of anger. "And so do I. You're not Roz. You're Chloe." Tears rolled down her cheeks. "Why did you let me call you Roz?" she demanded. "Why are you wearing her necklace? You think I'm stupid. Just because I get mixed up sometimes. You think you can play tricks on me."

"No, Gran," Chloe cried. "It wasn't like that at all. Honestly. Anna gave me the necklace for a keepsake, because I didn't have anything of my mother's. I didn't mean to confuse you. It's just that, well, you thought I was Roz so I — I went along with you, because you don't like me."

"Who said I don't like you?"

"*You* did, Gran. The day I arrived."

"Nonsense! I never said that." Indignation stopped Gran's tears. She gazed into the fireplace. Anna had filled the empty space with a vase of flowers. "Sometimes I say things I don't mean. They slip out. My tongue won't obey me. I don't know if you've noticed, but I have trouble with my memory. Of course, you don't understand. How could you?"

"Oh, but I do, Gran," Chloe burst out. "I have trouble with my memory, too. Before I came here I couldn't remember my mother, or you, or this house, or anything. That's why I came, to see if I could remember my mother."

"Poor child. I never had any trouble with remembering, when I was your age. They say it's because of the strokes, you know, but I think it was the shock." Gran was silent for a moment. "Something happened." She clutched at her skirt, arranging it and rearranging it over her knees. "I don't quite remember, but it was something terrible. Something Roz did. Sometimes I dream. Horrible dreams. You can't stop dreams, you know, however much you want to." Gran's eyes were haunted and grief stricken.

"I know, Gran," Chloe said. "I have bad dreams, too." The room seemed to be full of memories, like a ballroom full of ghostly dancers moving silently between the curved legs of the mahogany furniture, skimming over the hardwood floor and the Chinese carpet. Dancers whose faces Chloe couldn't quite make out. Tears of sympathy came to her eyes. "I'm sorry. I'll take the necklace off."

"No, no, my dear. Don't cry. It's all right." Gran gently pulled Chloe's head down onto her lap and stroked her hair. "It had something to do with you,

you see, all the heartache. First poor Roz and the dreadful thing she did, then your father taking you away like that. I don't think he meant to be cruel, but it was hard on Anna. I was afraid you'd make her miserable all over again, do you see? But I was wrong. She's happy now you've come. And I'm glad you're here, Chloe. I've got it right, haven't I? You're Chloe. You know, I think I'm beginning to get things straight at last."

Chapter Eleven

Gran had fallen into a light sleep after Chloe brought her some tea. While she waited for Gran to wake, or Anna to come home, Chloe tried to make some sense of the bits of information Gran had let drop. The thing Gran couldn't quite remember would be Roz's suicide, of course. Suicide would be even more shocking to a person of Gran's generation than it was to her own. But what had that got to do with her? *Something to do with you . . .* was what Gran had said. But what? What had Anna left out when she talked about it? Chloe felt as if she was back to the same old puzzle.

Overhead, the floor creaked. Chloe lifted her head to listen. The creaks didn't sound like the random complaints made by an old house. They sounded like someone moving across the floor. Chloe became aware of her own heart beating. She nudged her grandmother awake. "Did you hear anything, Gran?" she whispered. "There's a creaking noise upstairs."

Another creak.

"It's only Roz," Gran murmured. "Sometimes I hear her moving about up there. Once I saw her, but it was only a glimpse. I wish she'd come down, so that I could tell her I still love her. It doesn't matter what your child does, you know, you still love her. You can't help it." Tears came to her eyes again. "My old legs won't carry me upstairs anymore."

A shiver ran between Chloe's shoulder blades. Reason might tell her there was no such thing as ghosts, but Gran had come close to freaking her out. And even if it wasn't ghosts, the alternate explanation — someone in the house — didn't reassure her.

The noise above came again, like footsteps stealthily creeping along the upstairs hall. Real feet, not ghostly ones. Chloe tensed. She was in charge here. She had to find out what was going on. And she must not scare Gran. Her heart was doing flips. So was her stomach.

"I'm going upstairs to see if maybe Anna came in and somehow we didn't hear her," she whispered. "I'll be right back." Of course it was only Anna, she told herself. So why was she whispering? She wished she could pick up the poker, but Gran would notice and ask what she was doing. Noiselessly she closed the door of the living room behind her and crept into the front hall.

At the foot of the stairs she paused. The upstairs hallway was dark. There were so many hallways in this house, so many nooks and crannies where an intruder might hide, ready to jump out at her as she passed. No way was she going up there. She looked up and called hopefully, "Anna?"

No answer. The creaks stopped. She waited. Perhaps it had all been her imagination. Should she phone and ask Danny and his dad to come over? But if she had only imagined a burglar, she'd look like such an idiot . . . No, she'd already made enough of a fool of herself in Danny's boat. She wasn't going to do it again.

As the silence lengthened, she grew bolder. Gran's brass-handled walking stick was in the umbrella stand. It would make a good weapon. First she opened the front door, the better to make her escape, or let the burglar escape — either way she was not going to be trapped in the house with him — then she began to creep up the stairs. If only the darned things wouldn't squeak! After every squeak she stopped to listen. Nothing. Near the top she stopped, her back to the wall.

She planned her method of attack. She'd go to the top stair, then reach around the wall and snap on the light. If there *was* someone there, he'd be taken by surprise and probably run for it. Or was it a he? Not necessarily. She suddenly thought of Mrs. Bass. But why? Maybe because Danny had called her creepy, and the sounds were of someone creeping.

Her back still to the wall, Chloe stood on the top stair. It was now or never. Cautiously she slid her hand around the corner. Felt for the light switch. Her hand found someone else's, a hand that did not move. It felt smooth and cool.

Chloe screamed. She half ran, half fell down the stairs.

Gran limped into the hallway. "What's wrong?" she cried.

"Gran, there's someone upstairs. Go back inside." As quickly as she dared Chloe hustled Gran into the living room and wedged a chair under the door handle. Then she grabbed the phone and called Danny.

He and his father were there in minutes. Chloe heard their pickup come along the road, turn and roar down the Kenyons' private lane. Chloe ran to the door to let them in, then stayed with Gran while Mr. Wickel and Danny went upstairs to investigate. They were still there when Anna and Dr. Como came home.

"Chloe! What happened?" Anna cried. "Is it Mother? Mother, are you all right?"

"She's okay," Paul Wickel reassured her. "Chloe thought she heard someone upstairs, but there's no sign of anyone now. Did you hear anyone run downstairs and out the door, Chloe?"

Chloe shook her head.

"These old houses are full of noises," Paul Wickel said. "It's not hard to imagine footsteps."

"You don't imagine the feel of someone's hand," Chloe said, upset. He was making her sound stupid.

Anna turned pale. "You saw a *hand?*"

"I didn't see it. I felt it," Chloe said.

"Oh, my God!" Anna's exclamation was a horrified whisper. "Then there *was* someone in the house."

Paul Wickel shook his head. "I don't think so, Anna. There's no sign of a broken window, and the back door is still locked."

"But I didn't imagine it," Chloe insisted. "Gran heard someone, too."

"Only Roz," Gran said.

Anna looked as if she might faint. "Mother! Please!"

Dr. Como put his hand on her shoulder. "Take it easy, Anna."

Danny broke the uncomfortable silence that followed. "Is anything missing?" he asked.

"I'll check." Anna jumped up and headed upstairs.

"Paul, before you go, will you and Danny help me look around outside?" Dr. Como asked. "We'd better check to see if the cottage is secure, too. Do you have flashlights?" Danny handed him one as they headed outside.

"Mother's jewellery hasn't been disturbed," Anna told Chloe when she came back. "There's nothing else of much value in the house, and everything else looks normal. Where are the men?"

"Checking out the cottage," Chloe said.

"Oh no! I'm sure there's no need for that." In spite of Anna's protests she looked agitated. "Why don't you sleep downstairs tonight?" she suggested to Chloe. "There's a chaise longue in my room."

Chloe shook her head. "No. I'll be okay." She was beginning to feel ashamed of herself for imagining things. Even the hand could probably be explained — she'd look at the wall later and see what was hanging on it. A soft sculpture perhaps, a wall hanging . . . ?

But when Anna came up to say goodnight after the men had left, Chloe was still dressed. "Someone's been in here," she told Anna. "I know I'm not very tidy, but I left things straighter than this." Her hand flew to her mother's necklace. It still hung around her neck. Good thing she hadn't left it in her drawer.

"It's mainly my sketch pads someone's been fooling with, but they don't seem to have taken anything."

"You mean our burglar was an art lover?" Anna teased.

Chloe didn't find Anna's attempt at a joke very convincing. "Um, Anna, does Mrs. Bass have a set of keys to this house?"

"Oh, come now, Chloe. Mrs. Bass is scrupulously honest, and anyway, she's in Vancouver."

"All I mean is, someone else might have got hold of them."

"I'll check the doors again," Anna said.

While she waited for Anna, Chloe decided to straighten things out. The room was a bit of a mess with clothes tossed around, not a bit like it was when she'd arrived. As she put something in her dresser drawer, she noticed a difference. The book was missing!

When Anna came back she looked relieved. "All secure. The door was still locked. Chloe, dear, you're not used to this house. Quite ordinary creaks could sound eerie to you. I really do think you must have been mistaken about — "

"Anna, there's something else," Chloe said. *"The Water Babies* is gone. Unless . . . well, did you by any chance borrow it?"

"No!" Anna was plainly shocked. "No, how could I? I — I didn't even know where you'd put it." She pulled herself together. "Chloe, are you sure? I mean, you could have misplaced it. Why would anyone want to take that old book?"

"Maybe it's a collector's item," Chloe said. "Are you sure about the keys?" Maybe Anna didn't want to throw suspicion on her friend by admitting she had a set of keys. "Our neighbours have our keys. You know — in case of emergencies. It's possible someone else might have got hold of yours."

"No, no, I'm sure . . . "

Chloe decided not to push it. At least she'd made Anna think. The sweat on Anna's upper lip made that plain.

Chapter Twelve

By the time Chloe went to see Danny at the marina the next morning, he and his father were already gone.

"They're working at our old place," Marg told her. "They've been at it since first light. I was just about to take them a bit of lunch." She nodded toward a cooler and two loaded baskets.

"I could take it for you," Chloe said. "I've got my driver's licence."

Marg looked grateful. "Good. You can take Danny's old bone-shaker. I'll tell you how to get there."

Chloe found the farm without a problem. Where the men were working the land was wide and flat. Ripe cornstalks stood against the clear blue sky. Danny saw the truck coming down the rutted path and came striding across the field. "Hey, what's this?" He grinned. "I was expecting another woman."

"I hope you're not too disappointed," Chloe said.

"No way."

The way he looked at her made that the understatement of the year. While he helped her unload the cooler and lunch basket she said, "About last night. I want you to know I'm not totally out to lunch. After you'd gone I went into my bedroom, and guess what? My things were all over the place. Someone had been going through my sketch pads, and a drawing of Gran I've been working on wasn't where I left it. And you know what, Danny? The *Water Babies* book was missing. I *didn't* imagine it. Someone *was* in the house."

Danny's eyes narrowed. "The Bass woman."

"That's what I thought, but Anna says she's away."

"Not anymore," Danny said. "I saw her this morning. I took Buck down to the beach real early, 'cause I knew I'd be gone all day. He went running across the rocks and along Kenyons' beach, so I followed him." He glanced at her and grinned sheepishly. "To be honest, I was hoping I might see you. I was throwing sticks into the lake for Buck to fetch, so my back was to Mrs. Bass's cottage, but as he came out of the water he pricked up his ears and barked. I glanced around to see what had got his attention and I saw someone disappear around the back of her cottage. She must have got back from her holiday last night, and taken a cab from the bus station, 'cause I didn't see her van. I'd tell Dad, but he already thinks I've got something against her."

"But you didn't see her last night when you guys were searching the grounds?"

"No. Maybe she saw us first. She probably hid out in the cottage and pretended not to be home. That would be just like her. We didn't check inside. The doors were locked."

Danny's father joined them for lunch and they dropped the subject.

"Any more problems at your grandmother's place overnight, Chloe?"

Mr. Wickel looked at her kindly, but Chloe knew he didn't believe there had been a burglar. She shook her head.

He nodded. "Well, you did the right thing to call us," he said. "Better to be safe than sorry."

Chloe had set their lunch out on the shady side of the truck. Beyond the patch of shade, heat waves shimmered over the cut field. The heat silenced even the birds. A bee's drone faded into the distance. After lunch Mr. Wickel lay back, his hat over his eyes, and dozed. Danny stretched out, gazing at the sky and chewing on a straw.

Chloe wanted to stay there all afternoon, wrapped in the silence, close to Danny. He smelled as warm and as sweet as the fresh-cut corn. When he reached for her hand her heart felt as if it was going to rise into the sky like one of those hot-air balloons. Was she falling in love? Was this how it felt? She'd always looked down her nose at girls who flipped out over boys. She liked Danny — a lot — she already knew that. He wasn't like any other boy she'd ever met. But "in love"? Surely it couldn't be happening to her so fast.

Before she could follow the thought far enough

Paul Wickel sat up. "Well," he said, "back to work, Danny." Chloe got up too, to gather up the dirty cups, empty thermos flasks and crumpled wrappings and take them back to the marina.

"Thank you, Chloe. That was a big help." Marg said, beginning to load the dishwasher. "I thought we were all finished with visitors for the season, so I started stock-taking in the shop, but I just had a phone call. There's a family coming in a few hours and I've got to get one of the cottages ready."

Chloe looked at Marg's perspiring face. "I could help," she said.

"That's real kind, Chloe. Thank you. I could use an extra pair of hands."

Companionably, each carrying a load of clean linen, they walked through the old orchard to one of the cottages and started on the beds. Marg opened a sheet and flung one side across to Chloe. "You'll be going back to Edmonton pretty soon, I guess. School will be starting."

"I might stay here a bit longer."

"Oh? Anna would like that."

Chloe blushed. "D'you think so? I thought so, but I wasn't sure. Of course, I'd have to get Dad's permission, and make sure it's okay with Anna. I mentioned to her that I might ask Dad, and I've written him. She seemed kind of glad I wanted to, but . . . I don't know — I almost wondered if she hoped Dad would say no. He and Anna don't get along."

"I know," Marg said, tucking in a sheet. "It's too bad."

"Dad shouldn't have taken me away and not told

Anna and Gran where I was all those years. It wasn't fair."

"We don't know all the circumstances, Chloe," Marg said. "Don't be too quick to judge."

Surprised, Chloe followed Marg into the next bedroom. She'd expected Marg to be on Anna's side. "What circumstances?"

"Well, for one thing, your dad had been through a lot. First your mother's illness, then her death. Also, the local gossips didn't help. You know how it is. Since there was no body, there was no way of proving beyond any doubt that she took her own life, though it seemed pretty obvious to most people. Then we have the beautiful twin — you know, a ready-made eternal triangle — and the gossips put two and two together to make five. There was no truth to it whatever, of course. But I don't blame your father for wanting to get away."

"You mean people thought Dad and Anna . . . ?"

"Anna would never have done anything to hurt Roz," Marg said, answering Chloe's unspoken question. "She really loved her sister. I don't think it's possible for ordinary people to understand how close identical twins feel to one another."

Chloe nodded. But if Anna and Roz were so close, why did Anna always seem so reluctant to talk about her sister? Anna wasn't as bad as Dad, but still, there were so many questions left unanswered.

"Mrs. Wickel, why was my mother's body never found, d'you think? Didn't they look for her?" It was the worst part of her recurring nightmare — the thought of her mother under the water, trapped. And that it was her fault.

"This is a logging area," Marg began. "You've seen the log booms on the other side of the lake. A body could get trapped under the logs for a long time. Or, for that matter, tangled in the reeds. There are lots of reed beds around the lake. That's my theory, anyway, for what it's worth."

Chloe sank onto the unmade bed. The water . . . the weeds . . . by now there would only be bones left, white, water-washed bones . . .

Marg glanced over and saw Chloe's face. "Oh, I'm sorry, sweetie, I should have kept my dumb theories to myself. Now I've upset you."

"It's — no, it's okay," Chloe said. Partly to quieten her own imagination, and partly to put Marg at ease again, she added quickly, "Were Anna and my mother really so hard to tell apart?"

"They sure were." Marg handed Chloe a duster and began mopping the floor. She appeared glad of an excuse to talk about happier times. "I remember we did a play once in high school. It was one of those comedies by some old English playwright. We all had to dress up in period clothes — made them ourselves. Anna and Roz were the wife and her maid. They'd go in and out dressed in identical costumes and get the other characters thoroughly confused and mad at each other. In a play like that — where the humour depends on someone getting away with pretending to be someone else — the audience has to imagine that the two actors are impossible to tell apart. Usually, it's hard to believe. But with Roz and Anna there was no problem. Even their voices sounded the same."

"But Anna said Roz was right-handed and she's left. Didn't some people catch on to that?"

Marg smiled. "That didn't help much when they wanted to fool people, believe me. They both learned to use the other hand pretty well. When they wanted to give substitute teachers a hard time they'd start off using one hand and she'd think she'd got them straight. Then they'd switch back to their natural hands. Of course they still sat in the same seats. The poor teacher would be so confused."

"I wonder if I used to be able to tell who was who," Chloe said. "It would be weird not knowing which one was your mother, wouldn't it?"

"I can't help you with that one," Marg said. "I honestly don't remember, but clothes would give you a clue, wouldn't they? They didn't often dress alike as adults. You'd see how your mother dressed in the morning and the rest of the day you'd recognize her at a glance. Besides, they wouldn't want to fool you. Even when we were young, I remember they'd quickly say, 'I'm Roz,' or 'I'm Anna' if a friend made a mistake — that is, unless they were playing some trick. They didn't make a big deal of it. Just helped us keep them straight."

"You said my mother was popular with boys," Chloe said. "Was Anna, too?"

Marg smiled. "Oh yes. She was never short of a date."

"Is there anything else you remember about my

mother?" Chloe asked. "Anything that happened when I was little, for example."

Marg shook her head. "I didn't see much of your mother and Anna when our children were small. After we left school we sort of drifted apart. The twins went off to university while I married a farmer and started a family. Your parents lived in Calgary for awhile after they were married, so they were only out here for holidays. Occasionally we'd bump into one another in the summer, but on the whole our lives took different directions."

"Oh." Chloe frowned. What had seemed like a promising line of inquiry had come to a dead end.

Chapter Thirteen

When Chloe got home there was a woman talking to Anna. Sheltered by the high fence surrounding the deck at the side of the house, and engrossed in their conversation, the two women didn't hear Chloe come down the path.

"How could you be so careless?" Anna's tone was not so much angry as anguished. "I thought we had everything taken care of. Now what are we going to do? If Chloe were to find out . . . "

"Just get rid of her," the other woman said.

"But I don't *want* to get rid of her." Anna's voice was almost a wail.

"Frankly, I don't see any alternative. It's one or the other."

Breathlessly, Chloe crept back up the path. If they discovered the subject of their conversation eavesdropping it would be so embarrassing. Noisily heading down it again, she called out, "Hi, Anna," as though she'd just arrived. "I'm home."

Anna gave a little start. "Chloe! I thought you

were at Wickels'." She gave Chloe a quick glance, as though wondering how much she'd overheard, then, recovering, said, "I'd like you to meet Mrs. Bass. Mrs. Bass, this is my niece, Chloe."

Chloe gave Mrs. Bass a quick nod. So Danny had been right! The sculptor *was* here. But she wasn't keeping her presence a secret — at least, not today. A van, presumably hers, stood in the driveway. She must have hidden the van last night and made it look as if she'd just arrived today.

"How do you do," Mrs. Bass said.

Her handshake was firm and strong, her hand rough, not like the hand Chloe remembered from last night. Of course, last night she'd only touched it for a second, and then only the back of it. Mrs. Bass's whole body was firm and strong. She was a big woman, but muscular, not fleshy. Chloe found her slightly intimidating.

"I — I hope you had a good holiday," she managed.

"It wasn't a holiday. I was away on business." Mrs. Bass didn't smile.

Not an easy woman to like, Chloe thought. As usual when she was ill at ease, she started to talk non-stop. "I hear you're a sculptor," she said. "I'm very interested in art, but I've never tried sculpting — oh, except in clay — but stone seems very hard." She blushed at her accidental pun. "I mean, challenging."

"I like stone," Mrs. Bass said.

Forgetting Danny's comments on Mrs. Bass's unsociable nature, Chloe added, "Could I see some of your work sometime?"

"There isn't much around right now. I've just had a show in Vancouver. It almost sold out."

Anna jumped into the conversation. "I'm sorry, Chloe, but Mrs. Bass doesn't have time. She's going back to Vancouver. She only came back for something she'd forgotten."

Mrs. Bass nodded. "That's right. I left a piece that the gallery needs — in view of the success of the show. I probably won't be back here until after you've gone." She turned away. "I'd better get back to the cottage, Anna. I might need your help later to load that piece."

"I could — " Chloe began.

"No. No. We don't want to drop it. Anna's used to helping."

Danny was right, Chloe decided. Mrs. Bass was not strong on personal warmth. Anna, gesturing nervously, accompanied Mrs. Bass to the end of the garden path. Chloe wondered whether Mrs. Bass intimidated her too.

She strained to hear what they were saying. Unfortunately, Anna's voice was light and didn't carry.

Some of Mrs. Bass's deeper tones were easier to pick up. " . . . won't be easy . . . stubborn as a mule . . . have to choose between them . . . my advice . . . up to you . . . "

Anna was nodding, but her reply was inaudible. As soon as Mrs. Bass headed off for the cottage Anna returned, shoulders slumped. Then she straightened up and forced herself to look cheerful. "It's so warm today," she said, "I thought we'd barbecue and have supper out here. The trees keep it cool. We mustn't waste the last days of your holiday."

Chloe looked at Anna's face, at the deep shadows under her eyes. It sounded as though Anna meant to take Mrs. Bass's advice and send her packing before school started again.

"You know," said Grandma Kenyon when they were eating dessert, "there's something missing from this apple pie. Mercy me, I just remembered. I forgot the cheese. As your daddy used to say, 'Apple pie without cheese is like a kiss without a squeeze.'" She chuckled. Then, as Anna started to get up she said, "No, sit still. I'll get it."

"Your grandma's much livelier lately," Anna said to Chloe. "I think she enjoys your company."

And what about you? Chloe wondered. You told Mrs. Bass you didn't want to get rid of me, yet you look as if just being around me makes you nervous.

"It's funny I haven't had a letter from Dad yet," she said, trying to work her way around to the subject of staying. "I know the mail's slow, but I thought I'd have heard by now."

"Oh well," Anna smiled. "This way we get to enjoy your company for a bit longer."

That confirmed it. No matter what Dad's letter might say, Anna had already made up her mind. She was going to take Mrs. Bass's advice.

By the time they had finished supper, the sun was sinking behind the mountains. The slopes were dark, their rounded peaks outlined against an aquamarine sky. Across the lake, sunlight still bathed the upper slopes, turning the treetops to gold and the upper meadows into a pattern of variegated greens.

Feeling the need to make conversation, Chloe said, "Funny how we always think of the sun rising or sinking, when really we're the ones doing the moving."

"Which only goes to show," said Anna, grudgingly, "that things aren't always what they seem." Immediately, she seemed to regret her comment, blushed furiously and brushed it off with a nervous laugh.

What was wrong with Anna? Chloe wondered. She was always a little jumpy, but now she was a mass of nerves, as if at any moment she expected to feel a hand on her shoulder. What was making her so terrified? Did it have anything to do with whoever had been sneaking around Chloe's room last night?

Chloe could find no answers. Only one thing was certain. Whatever had happened last night had upset Anna more than she would admit.

Chapter Fourteen

Late the following evening, just as Chloe was getting ready for bed, Danny phoned.

"How about a moonlight swim?" he asked.

"Sounds cold."

He chuckled. "Chicken! The air's cooler, so the water will feel warmer. It's all relative. Are you coming?"

"Okay."

"I'll pick you up in fifteen minutes."

"Take something warm along for afterwards," Anna said when Chloe told her. "The air feels cold when you come out." She flitted about straightening cushions and picking up magazines — anything to delay going to bed.

What's she really worried about? Chloe wondered. Why can't she say? All the same, she took Anna's advice and grabbed her summer jacket and two thick towels. No sense feeling cold. "Here's Danny," she said when she heard his truck roaring along the road. "Don't wait up."

Instead of driving back to the marina and the familiar jetty, Danny continued along the road. "There's a little bay farther along," he said. "My brother and I discovered it. The bottom drops off pretty fast so you don't have to wade out so far before you can swim."

They reached the spot he was aiming for, a place where the shoulder widened barely enough to let him park the pickup off the road. A stand of evergreens hid the lake from view. Danny made for the trees.

"Wait," Chloe cried. "Where are you going?" Although close to full, the moon was still low in the sky and the trees threw long shadows. Shoulder to shoulder, the shadows gave the impression of an impenetrable black forest. "We can't go through there," she protested. "It's too dark to see where we're going."

Danny waved a flashlight. "I came prepared. I used to be a boy scout."

"Evergreens have needles like cat's claws," Chloe protested. "I don't know about you, but I'm not about to get scratched to pieces."

"There's a path," Danny said, grinning. "Trust me."

"Well, anyway, I think I'll wear my jacket," Chloe said. She was doing up the zipper when a loud crack broke the silence of the night. Startled, she clutched Danny's arm. "What was *that?*" she whispered, her heart pounding. "It sounded like a gunshot. Someone's in there."

For a moment Danny seemed as startled as she

was, then he relaxed. "It was only a branch breaking off, or maybe a rotten trunk snapping. Funny how loud it sounded. I suppose it's because the night is so quiet."

"Why would it suddenly snap?" Chloe asked. "It's not as if there's much wind blowing."

Danny shrugged. "They get rotten enough and they just go," he said. "Come on, give me your bag. How come you brought so much stuff?"

"Anna said it might be cold."

All Danny carried was a towel. He shifted it to one hand and lifted Chloe's bag with the other.

"Danny, there are bears in the hills, aren't there? They might come down to the lake to drink. They'd think they were safe from people at night. D'you know what I think? That tree or branch was broken by a bear looking for bugs. What if we stumble across it in the dark?"

"I'll hit it over the head with my flashlight."

"Very funny," she said.

"Come on, city girl. Here, you carry my towel. I need a hand for the flashlight."

After the first few steps Danny made a ninety-degree turn, then another. To Chloe's amazement, they did seem to be following a path. Even so, she stumbled, the pool of light dancing about, confusing her.

Danny seemed excited. "I bet you'd never have found this path on your own," he called over his shoulder. "My brother and I cut it when we were kids. Since he left home I've kept it up myself. Nobody else knows about it."

Chloe wished she could just relax and enjoy this time with Danny, but questions kept flitting through her mind. How could Danny be so sure nobody else knew about the path? What about the person who had been in Gran's house? This place would make a perfect hideout for some creepy guy. By now he would have heard her and Danny coming. Danny's truck didn't exactly purr, and they hadn't been whispering. Someone could be lurking behind a tree somewhere, waiting for his chance to murder them. She could see the headlines: TWO TEENAGERS KILLED IN B.C. FOREST. Her mouth dry with fear, she glanced behind. In the general blackness, there was no telltale shadow to betray a watcher in the trees. "Danny, stop," she whispered. "Listen." Something rustled in the undergrowth. "What's that?"

"I don't know. Some animal."

She wished he'd keep the flashlight steady so she could see where she was putting her feet. The pool of light made everything else darker by contrast. It was like walking through a black tunnel.

Chloe wasn't sure about it, but she thought there were snakes in B.C. A few were probably poisonous. Maybe that's what she'd heard slithering through the undergrowth. "Suppose one of us steps on a snake."

Danny chuckled again. "Not a chance. The snakes are all tucked up for the night under nice, warm rocks."

When Chloe accidentally kicked one of his heels, Danny yelped. Apologizing, she saw that they were coming out of the trees and the water was almost at their feet, across a strand of pebbles. The lake looked different at night. Not like water at all. More like a black hole, fallen from the sky, gleaming under the moon.

Danny turned off the flashlight and they waited for their eyes to get used to the dark.

Chloe gasped. Someone was lying on the beach, motionless, white in the moonlight, arms and legs spread-eagled. *Her body was never found . . .*

Danny noticed the expression on her face. "What's wrong?"

She managed to nod toward the body.

"That old pile of driftwood?"

"Driftwood?" she whispered. "Are you sure?"

"What else?"

Now that he pointed it out, she could see it was driftwood. "I thought . . . It looks so white."

"It's been in the water and then in the sun and got bleached. The moonlight makes it look whiter. Interesting shape, isn't it? Roots, most likely. Some people collect driftwood and turn it into planters and things. Do you want to take some home?"

"No," she said. "It would be like decorating your house with someone's skeleton. It still sort of gives me the creeps."

Danny shrugged. "I never knew anybody else who felt that way. Well, you don't have to take it. Come on."

As they began to walk along the beach, a dark shape swooped down on them, silent until its vast wings moved the air over their heads. Chloe screamed, pulling away from Danny and hugging her head. The breadth of the wings was monstrous. The draft of their passing lifted her hair.

"It's okay," Danny said, pulling her back into the crook of his arm. "It's only old Wol, the owl. That's his way of saying hi. He's quite a character. I'll show you his roost later."

Petrified, Chloe didn't move. "I want to go," she said, angry with Danny for not warning her about the owl.

"But we just got here."

Fear tightened like an iron band around Chloe's chest. She could hardly breathe. Another of her panic attacks was coming on. "Let's go to the jetty," she said. "There's something spooky about this place."

"Spooky?" He glanced up at the sky. "It's a bit cloudy and you can hear the tops of the trees creaking in the breeze, but I wouldn't call it spooky. You're just looking at it the wrong way. You don't have to be scared. I won't let anything happen to you. Honest."

Struggling to fight down her fear, Chloe had no breath to answer him. It was all very well for Danny to say she shouldn't be scared, but how was she to stop? Any minute now she was going to start hyperventilating and making an absolute idiot of herself.

"Come on. I'll find us a nice, steep bit of beach. No mud, I promise." Danny started off along the water's edge.

Afraid to be alone, she followed him, skirting the

pile of driftwood while trying not to look at it. The thump of her heart filled her whole body.

She couldn't go on. "Danny," she wailed. "Let's go back. Please."

"Chloe! You knew we were coming to swim. You promised. I'm going in. If you don't want to, you don't have to, but I didn't drive all the way out here not to swim."

She turned her back on him. Okay. She'd go sit in the truck. Maybe even drive it home and leave him to walk. Serve him right.

She took a few steps and stopped. To get to the truck she'd have to walk back through the trees. She could almost feel an arm reaching out from between the trees, pinning her own arms to her sides, a hand covering her mouth. She wouldn't be able to move. Wouldn't be able to scream. Sweat soaked her shirt and made it cling, cold, to her back. She couldn't go to the truck on her own.

Danny was furiously stripping down to his swim trunks. "I never brought anyone here before," he said. "It was my secret. My special place. I thought you'd feel the same way I do about it." He waved his arm around. "Can't you see? The trees and . . . and the pebbles and . . . that driftwood, the water, everything. They all look different in the moonlight. Beautiful. Enchanted somehow. I wanted us to see it. Just the two of us. I wanted you to feel the way I do about it."

"Well, I don't. I'm scared."

"What? Of me? You think I brought you here to scare you?"

His voice broke and Chloe realized he was close to tears.

He turned away from her. "Just forget it. I'm going for a swim." He plunged in, swimming away from the beach.

Chloe huddled on the shore, hugging her legs, her forehead pressed against her knees. Danny would have to come out of the water sometime. If only he'd hurry, before something awful happened. She felt as if she were going to die. *Please come back, Danny. Please. Everything will be okay, if only you'll come out of the water. . .*

She looked up to see if her silent plea had reached him. He was gone. Frantic, she leaped to her feet, desperately searching the lake. She thought she heard the sound of wings and threw herself face down on the beach, clawing at the pebbles.

The wings passed, and then there was only the sound of the wind, and her own whimpering.

Eventually she sat up and looked around. Danny was back, just wading out of the water. She followed him along the beach.

He pulled up beside her bag. "You still here?" he said.

Chloe opened her mouth to tell him not to be such a jerk, but the wrong words came out. "I couldn't help it," she wailed. "I was really scared before. I don't mean just of this place." Her voice quivered. She tried to take a deep breath. "Danny, there's something wrong with me." Tears began to slide down her face.

"Hey . . . Hey, take it easy." He reached out to touch her wet face, then fumbled in her beach bag for a tissue. "Here, use this," he said, handing her a towel. "You're okay. Really."

"How can you say that? After the way I behaved tonight, and the way I freaked out on the boat. It's not normal. *I'm* not normal. I didn't want to tell you before, but I get these panic attacks — for no reason."

Danny sat down beside her. "Well . . . Okay . . . So you're scared of water."

"I used to be," Chloe agreed. "But it's not that. I made myself learn to swim."

"Sure," Danny said. "You can swim, but anybody can see you're not really comfortable. You go stiff as a board."

It wasn't a very flattering description. Even in her misery, she wished he hadn't noticed.

"I think you have a phobia," Danny went on. "Like some people are afraid of heights, and some freak out in small spaces. When my cousin was a little kid he was afraid of small, furry animals. He'd scream like a maniac if he got anywhere near one."

"But he got over it?"

"Sure. First they got him used to furry toys, then to one of those mechanical puppies and finally to a real rabbit. He just had to learn that small, furry things weren't going to hurt him."

"So you don't think I'm . . . abnormal?"

"No," he said, "but I think you've got to find out what's bothering you and face up to it, or you'll always have a problem. Maybe you should talk to a shrink or somebody. But if you want to spill your guts to an ordinary guy, well, hey, my couch is available, and the price is right."

"Thanks, Dr. Freud." Chloe tried to grin to convince him she was okay. But she wasn't. Call it a phobia if you like, she had a mental problem — no doubt inherited from her mother — and Danny knew it. Otherwise he wouldn't be talking about shrinks. He was trying to be kind, but he'd never really like her after this.

She looked over Danny's shoulder, at the sky. The moon had climbed higher, its light streaming over the trees, bringing them to life. Of course there was no one hiding here. The silent watcher existed only in her own imagination.

She followed Danny back to the truck, unable to shake off her feeling of melancholy. This was an old patch of forest where not only spruce, but fir, larch and cedar grew undisturbed. But how long before they were cut down, their beauty lost? They'd be like corpses piled high in a lumber yard, or bleached wooden bones piled on a beach . . . She gazed out the truck's window at the trees as they wound their way back along the road.

On the way home Danny seemed as thoughtful as she was. They hardly talked at all until they pulled up to Anna's house. Chloe felt the silence like an accusation. Couldn't he say *something* to make her feel less like a loser?

"I never told anyone about my problem before," she managed, before climbing out of the truck. "Thanks for listening, Danny."

He blushed furiously. "No problem. I'm sorry I got so mad. Okay? Listen, I'll see ya."

But he didn't say when. Chloe felt too miserable to ask.

That night she tossed and turned, not knowing which was harder to take, her loss of Danny's friendship — for she felt sure she had lost it — or the terror she had felt in that secluded bay. It had been so unexpected, so out of her control.

"There's nothing to fear but fear itself." That's the saying Joyce would have used. But Chloe didn't care about famous sayings. Fear wasn't a nothing. It was terrible. Nobody wanted to feel like that, like they were going to die of fright.

She spent the night tossing, and hardly slept.

Chapter Fifteen

When Chloe came down to breakfast, she couldn't eat. She sat nibbling at a piece of toast, but it threatened to stick in her throat. To make matters worse, Grandma Kenyon was having a bad day.

"Anna, why did you make tea?" she asked fretfully. "I want coffee."

"But, Mother," Anna protested. "You said you'd like tea this morning."

"No, I didn't. You never listen to what I say. When you get old, nobody cares about you."

"Mother, you know that's not true," Anna said. "I'll make coffee if that's what you'd like." She picked up the coffee pot and whispered an aside to Chloe. "I invited Dr. Como to supper this evening, but maybe I'll have to cancel if she's like this."

"What're you whispering about?" Grandma Kenyon snapped.

"We were just saying we care about you a great deal, don't we, Chloe?" Anna turned to Chloe for support.

Chloe nodded.

Anna looked anxiously from Chloe to her un-eaten toast. "Is something wrong? You don't seem yourself this morning."

Chloe burst into tears. "Oh, Anna," she said, "I hurt Danny's feelings last night and I'm sure he never wants to see me again."

Torn between her mother's needs and Chloe's, Anna turned from the sink to Chloe and back to the sink again. "Just let me get Mother's coffee started." Then she sat down beside Chloe and drew her close. "Now, what's all this about Danny?"

"Why do people keep mumbling behind my back?" Grandma Kenyon grumbled. "I want my coffee."

"Please, Mother, try to be patient," Anna said. "Chloe's upset. She has a problem with her friend Danny."

"Leave him alone, and he'll come home, bringing his tail behind him," Gran said, giggling.

"It isn't funny," Chloe said, hurt.

"No, of course it isn't," Anna said. "Mother, stop it."

It was the first time Chloe had ever heard Anna speak sharply to Gran.

Anna turned back to Chloe. "Maybe it's for the best if you and Danny see a little less of each other. I was getting a bit worried where it all might lead. You've only known him for a couple of weeks."

Appalled, Chloe stared at Anna. "I thought you liked him."

"I do. I think a lot of Danny. It's just . . . " Anna

waved her hand helplessly. ". . . you're both so young. And I see girls your age, still at school, fall for a boy, ruin their education. You know . . . Usually it's the girl who pays, but Danny's a conscientious boy. He'd suffer too." Anna took hold of Chloe's shoulders. "It would be better if you did go home, Chloe. I think I felt that all along, but I wanted to keep you here for my own selfish reasons. I hope you don't mind my talking frankly like this. But I feel I have to." She sighed. "You do understand, don't you?"

Chloe drew away from her. Why was Anna suddenly so anxious to be rid of her? She felt sure it wasn't all to do with Danny. He was just an excuse. But . . . If Danny didn't like her as much as she liked him, any longer, she might as well go home. It wasn't as if her trip here had answered any of her real questions about her mother anyway. That whole plan had flopped. And it was clear that having her around set her aunt on edge. Maybe . . . maybe it would be easier, back home in Edmonton, to forget Danny. A fresh flood of tears overwhelmed her.

Anna hugged her. "Don't cry, Chloe. Please don't. I hate to see you so upset." Anna's own eyes had tears in them. "I know how you feel, believe me."

Chloe tensed up. Anna was wrong. Nobody knew how she felt.

As Anna got up to pour Grandma Kenyon's coffee Chloe watched her bustling about, trying to satisfy Gran. Now that I've broken up with Danny, she thought, what if I end up like Anna, alone? Was that what had happened to Anna? Never able to find anyone to love the way she'd loved Dad? Until now?

Chloe felt a rush of sympathy for Anna. Maybe she should think about *her* for a change. She wiped her eyes and turned to her grandmother. "Gran," she said, "we thought we'd ask Dr. Como to supper today. Won't that be nice?"

"No," said Grandma Kenyon. "He's always asking me questions. Questions, questions, questions. I don't want him here."

Anna's face fell.

Before Anna could give in Chloe said, "If you don't want to have supper with Dr. Como, Gran, you and I can eat in the kitchen."

"I don't like to eat dinner in the kitchen," Gran said.

"In that case, I'm afraid we'll just have to eat with Dr. Como," Chloe said.

Gran gave Chloe a sidelong glance. "We'll see."

Through the morning Chloe helped Anna with the housework and then took Gran for a little walk. After lunch, when Gran went to lie down for her afternoon nap, Chloe and Anna started on the supper. Just as Anna was washing the bowls they'd used to make a cake, the phone rang. Hoping it might be Danny, Chloe reached for the phone, but Anna snatched the receiver, sudsy hands and all.

I might have known, Chloe thought. Anna had a thing about answering her own phone, as if she was afraid it might explode in anyone else's hands.

Lately she'd been jumpier than ever about it.

But it wasn't Danny anyway, just someone for Anna. Since Anna was so concerned about answering her own phone, Chloe wondered if she should leave the room, but the caller didn't seem to be Dr. Como, or anyone interesting. It sounded more like someone trying to arrange an outing for seniors and wanting to include Gran. Chloe got on with peeling the vegetables.

Dr. Como arrived early. "We didn't have time to talk last time we met," he said, shaking Chloe's hand, "but I feel I know you. Anna has told me a lot about you."

Peter Como was of medium height and slight build. Chloe got the feeling he was intensely interested in her. What had Anna told him? Excusing herself, she went to help Grandma Kenyon get dressed after her nap. She wondered what kind of mood her grandmother would be in. She searched through the closet until she found a royal blue dress for Gran to wear. "I love this colour," she said. "It's so pretty with your silver hair."

"Then I'll wear it. Find me my pin, dear — the silver filigree with the diamond chips. It's the one Albert bought me on our trip to New York."

When Gran made her appearance in the living room Dr. Como greeted her with the same warmth he'd shown Chloe. Chloe might have found his frank gaze rude if it hadn't been for the smile that softened both his mouth and his eyes. The smile seemed to charm Gran, too. She gave Dr. Como her hand and he held it between both of his. It was quite obvious she liked him. There'd be no question of eating in the kitchen.

Anna, carrying a tray, joined them, and passed around drinks and nibbles. She was dressed in white, her red-gold hair once again freed from its bun, her skin almost as white as the dress. The effect was angelic, Chloe thought, and yet it made her feel queasy for some reason. "Is something wrong, Chloe?" Anna asked. Her hand flew to her dress. "Did I forget to button something?"

Chloe blushed. She hadn't realized she was staring. "No, I . . . I was just admiring your dress," she stammered.

Anna chuckled. "This old thing? I've had it for years. It shows you, if you keep something long enough, it comes back into fashion. But I'm glad you like it."

Why did I lie? Chloe asked herself. I don't like it at all. All that white — it makes me think of death somehow, like that tangle of driftwood I thought was bones . . .

To take her mind off her gloomy thoughts she surreptitiously watched Dr. Como and Anna. He's in love with her, she thought. And I bet Anna's in love with him. Is it shyness that makes her try to hide her feelings, or a sense of duty toward Gran, or what? She's so tense all the time. Why can't she let herself be happy?

"Why are you picking at your food like that, child?" Gran complained. "There's nothing wrong with it."

"I'm just not hungry, Gran," Chloe said. "Maybe it's the heat."

After supper, when she had taken care of the cleaning up, she felt reluctant to join the others. It was hard to see Anna and Dr. Como together, when all she could really think about was how she'd blown it with Danny. "If you don't mind," she said to them, "I think I'll go up to bed. I didn't sleep much last night."

They nodded and wished her sweet dreams, not seeming to mind at all.

Through the bedroom window Chloe could see the lake. The water had ripples on it tonight, their tips touched by the light of the full moon.

Danny was right. Moonlight did give things a special beauty, like an etching. Chloe sighed. How could I have been so stupid last night? I spoiled everything, and all because of a totally unreasonable fear. I've got to get over it before it ruins my life. I have to prove to myself there's nothing at all to be afraid of. But how?

She lay there for awhile before the answer came to her. It was simple, really. Why not start now? Just a short swim. Nothing too challenging.

She almost called Danny to see if he'd like to go with her, but changed her mind. If she had another panic attack she could come back to the house and nobody would know, not even Danny. Not that she was going to. Tomorrow she could tell him what she'd done and he'd see she wasn't a total flake and that he didn't have to feel sorry for her. Maybe things would even get back to normal between them.

She collected a couple of towels and changed into her swimsuit. There's really nothing to it, she told herself as she crept down the back stairs and let herself out.

Chapter Sixteen

Chloe stood at the edge of the water, gazing at the lake. Tonight, with waves tipped by moonlight, the water looked almost light-hearted, inviting her in to join the fun. Even so, a part of her drew back. Quickly, before she could change her mind, she stripped down to her swimsuit, dropped her jeans, T-shirt and towels in a pile on the beach, and waded in.

The bottom felt soft under her feet, but Danny had said it did that for a few metres and then it was okay. She fought the impulse to run back to shore and took a deep breath to steady herself. Only a few steps, and then the water would be deep enough to swim and the bottom wouldn't matter. She hurried forward and flung herself into the water.

It felt fine. Jubilant, she turned on her back and let herself float. The moon made the night almost as bright as day. Relax, she told herself, remembering Danny's comment about her stiffness. She looked up at the sky. The edge of a cloud passed across the moon. It was beautiful. She'd try and draw it just like this, tomorrow, the way she remembered it right now.

But in a few moments she began to feel cool. Better swim. In an effort to get warm she swam in one direction, then turned and went in the other. She was still cold. Her teeth refused to stop chattering.

She decided it was okay to go back, and struck out for the shore. Anyway, she'd proved she could swim at night. She couldn't wait to see Danny's face when she told him tomorrow.

She lifted her head and looked for the shore. It seemed as far away as before. She hadn't realized she'd come so far. The wind must be blowing off the land, against her. She would have a hard swim back, but she told herself to stay calm.

A wave splashed into her face, filling her nose and mouth. Panting, she kept treading water, and shook her head to get the water off her face. Another wave hit her face. The moon disappeared behind a cloud and left her in the dark. Another wave, and she swallowed water. Before she could draw a breath, water totally covered her head. She couldn't breathe. She flailed out, fighting for air.

"Mommy!" she cried. "Mommy. Help me." At first she wasn't sure who was shouting, then she knew it was herself. Water covered her face again and she couldn't shout. Couldn't move.

This was how it had happened, long ago . . . The shock of remembering made her open her eyes under the water. Instead of soft moonlight, the sun shone hot and bright. Above her, through shimmering waves, her mother stood watching. She was dressed in white, her skin as pale as her dress. Her white arms reached down. Chloe grabbed, tried to use the white arms as ropes to haul herself up. But instead of helping, Mommy pushed her down. Terrified, Chloe fought like a wildcat. Water filled her eyes and nose. She couldn't breathe. She had to get to the air above! Help, Mommy! Help!

Mommy gazed down, but her eyes were all wrong. They looked like glass, like the eyes in Chloe's dollies. Mommy couldn't see Chloe, only something or someone far away. Her lips moved, as if she were singing to herself, but Chloe couldn't hear the song.

She wanted to shout, "Mommy, look at me. I'm here," but she couldn't breathe. Through the water, Mommy's face wavered, changing shape, like in one of those funny mirrors at the fair. Mommy just nodded, waved. Why? Was she saying good-bye? Didn't Mommy want her? Didn't Mommy love her? What had she done?

For a moment she was able to grasp one of Mommy's arms and stay above water.

"Go, Chloe, darling. Go," Mommy urged. She looked scared. "Go to Mrs. Doasyouwouldbedoneby. She'll take care of you. Go to Tom and the others. It's not safe here. Swim away. Swim down under the water, as fast as you can."

But Chloe couldn't swim under the water. She wasn't like Tom. Tom was a boy in a story. In a story, people could do anything. Chloe wasn't in a story, and she couldn't breathe. Why didn't Mommy know that? What was wrong with her?

Chloe fought to get free. Below her, horrible things waited to grab her. Lobsters with cruel claws and beady eyes, and jelly-like things with grasping arms, crawling insects with a hundred legs and long, waving horns. She fought to get away from them, but she was so tired, too tired to struggle anymore. She closed her eyes and gave up . . .

Cold air hit her in the face like a slap. She gasped, gulping air. Too terrified to think, she thrashed about in panic. Again, water covered her face. Blindly she fought to escape. Found the air. Lost it again. In her panic she was unable to time her breathing. Instead of air, she gulped water. Gagged. She was getting weaker. Less able to fight her way to the surface.

"Chloe. Chlo-eee. Where are you?"

Someone was calling her. The moon came out from behind the clouds, lighting the shoreline and the mountain peaks. She turned over onto her back, trying to calm herself enough to manage a simple float. The air felt cool on her face.

"Chlo-eee."

Chloe turned her head. She could see a woman standing on the beach in the moonlight. A woman dressed in white. *White* . . . What was her mother doing there?

But it wasn't her mother. Her mother was dead. And she wasn't a little girl anymore. She was sixteen, swimming in the lake, at night, alone.

Now she knew.

All these years I've been wrong. I didn't cause my mother's death. It was the other way around. My mother tried to drown *me,* when I was just a little girl.

Chloe realized she was sobbing. No tears, just great sobs shaking her chest. No, surely not my mother. She sobbed again. I must be worthless, no good somehow . . .

No! It can't be true. I made a mistake. It wasn't my mother. It must be someone else. Anna . . . Anna had a white dress too . . .

Roz and Anna, so alike. How could I know which one for sure? No wonder her white dress made me feel ill. That's Anna on the beach there, looking for me. She might try to do something to me again. Now, when it would be so easy.

Chloe shook her head. Must escape. Must get out of the water as fast as I can, before Anna finds me.

Fear gave her a burst of strength. She turned back onto her stomach and kicked, leaping for the beach like a salmon at a waterfall.

But there were still the waves. She wasn't going to make it. The frantic churning of her arms was only making her more and more tired. Desperately weary, she sank. Her knees brushed the bottom, taking her by surprise. She was in shallow water. On all fours she scrambled up to the beach, collapsed and rolled over onto her back, sobbing with relief.

When she could open her eyes, stars filled the sky. The empty beach lay moonlit around her. The night was silent.

Nearby, a door quietly opened and closed. Only a creak and a slight click gave it away. Someone was trying not to be heard. The cottage? Mrs. Bass! Were they in it together, Anna and Mrs. Bass?

Her heart racing with fear, Chloe struggled to her feet and staggered along the beach. A figure ran toward her, white in the moonlight. Chloe wanted to scream, but couldn't. She tried to run the other way, but her legs wouldn't move. Paralyzed with fear, like a rabbit caught in the glare of headlights, she waited helplessly until the figure in white reached her.

"Chloe! What happened? Oh, my God! Are you all right? I found your towels and jeans. Where's Danny?"

"I — I don't know."

"You came out here *alone?* What were you thinking of? Have you taken leave of your senses?" Anna grabbed Chloe's arm and shook her.

Chloe had never seen Anna like this — furious. But she's not mad with anger, Chloe realized. She's mad with fear. Like Dad a couple of times when he thought something had happened to her.

Anna got control of herself. "You're shivering. Here, put this towel around you. Let's run for the house before you get cold."

When they reached the house they found Gran in the kitchen wearing her dressing gown and slippers. "I've been all alone," she complained. "You said Dr. Como would stay with me, but he had to go. He got an emergency call. Where have you two been?"

128

"For a midnight swim, Mother," Anna said. She turned to Chloe. "Into the shower. Make it hot."

By the time Chloe came downstairs Anna had a fire burning in the wood stove. "Mother's gone to bed," she said. "I've made you some hot chocolate."

She had calmed down, and waited silently while Chloe swallowed a few sips before she started to speak. "Chloe, surely you know you shouldn't swim alone, especially at night. If I hadn't gone out for some fresh air and heard your cries . . . What happened? You got cramps, I suppose, and panicked?"

"Cramps? No," Chloe said. But panic, yes. It would be such a relief to talk about it. She took another sip of the hot chocolate. While it warmed her, she began to tell Anna about her panic attacks, and how Danny had said she had to face her fear. She explained how she thought she could do it, be able to swim without getting so scared, and then about the panic she couldn't control. "I almost lost it," she admitted.

She paused. Should she go on? There was all that stuff about her mother. Finally, she'd remembered. She wanted to tell Anna, but something stopped her. How could she tell anybody that her own mother had tried to drown her? Nobody would believe her. Least of all Anna. Anyway, how did she know for sure it was her mother? It could just as easily have been Anna. Anna, dressed in white, pale-skinned, her mother's identical twin . . .

But the other memory resurfaced, hitting Chloe like a wave. I called her Mommy. It *was* my mother

. . . My own mother . . . No wonder I couldn't remember her before. I wouldn't let myself.

The full horror of it began to penetrate Chloe's understanding. I was only a little kid. How could she? Oh, how could she?

And then another fear, seeping in. Will I turn out like her? Is there some unhealthy gene waiting for a chance to do its work on me? What kind of life have I got to look forward to?

Chloe's arms wrapped over her stomach; she rocked back and forth, back and forth. "Oh, help me," she moaned. "Won't somebody please help me?" Her moans turned into sobs.

"Chloe, dearest, stop. Please stop," Anna begged. "You're safe now. You're here in the house with me. Please, Chloe. You'll scare Mother." Anna sounded scared herself.

The noise was terrifying. Chloe wanted it to stop, too, but she had no control over the girl who was screaming.

Chapter Seventeen

When Chloe woke up the next morning she was not in her own bed but in Anna's, and saw that Anna had spent the night on the chaise longue. Slowly the events of the night before came back to her. To her surprise, she felt very calm. She supposed it was the effect of the pills Dr. Como had persuaded her to swallow when he returned in answer to Anna's call for help.

In spite of her calm, Chloe knew there was something she had to do, and do quickly, before the numbing effect of the pill wore off and the knowledge grew less bearable. She must tell Danny what she had remembered last night.

Without disturbing Anna, Chloe eased herself out of bed. She crept upstairs to use the shower and get dressed in her own room. Before leaving the house she wrote a note for Anna and set it on the kitchen table, to say she was going to see Danny.

Instead of going along the beach, she walked along the road to Danny's place. It was as if, by putting as much distance as possible between herself and the water, she could distance herself from the memories of last night. But even though she deliberately avoided looking down at the lake, her strategy failed. Again and again the scene replayed itself, like an old movie, and she saw her mother, dressed in white, looming over her. Tears filled Chloe's eyes. The road was a blur.

She found Danny in a clearing among the trees, using a saw on a pile of logs.

"Thought I'd get a head start on winter," he explained, nodding at the big stack.

Chloe sat on a tree stump and composed herself until Danny stopped to set a new length of log onto his sawhorses. "Danny," she said, gathering her courage. "There's something I have to tell you."

Frowning intently, Danny perched sideways on the log and gave her his full attention.

She told him about her swim the previous night, and the memories it had triggered. " . . . It was horrible. I was under the water and I wanted my mother to help me and she wouldn't." Despite the unnatural calm the tranquilizer was still making her feel, Chloe's words choked her.

As Danny started to speak, she shook her head. "No, let me finish." Taking a deep breath to steady her voice, she went on, "That time we were out in the boat and I acted so weird — I'm sure I was almost remembering then, only the way I saw it, I was looking down at *her* and *she* was drowning. But I had it the wrong way around. Really I was looking *up,* not down. You know that book, *The Water*

Babies? I think my mother must have gone way overboard with that story, sort of like she wanted to send me to live under the water like Tom. Remember your mother said that my mother had collected so many copies of that book? I'd wondered why, but now . . . well, I think I know. Oh, Danny. Don't you see? My mother had lost her mind. She was so sick, she almost drowned me!" A sob came to her throat.

Danny stood up, but again Chloe stopped him with a shake of her head. "Great genes I've got. Right?" she said, trying to steady her voice. "If you don't want to have anything more to do with me, I'll understand."

She had thought she was numb, but her words brought another outpouring of tears. Turning away from Danny, she wiped her eyes and blew her nose, then looked back at him. Danny wasn't saying anything. Why was he so silent? If only he would tell her quickly how he felt, before she turned to total mush.

"Are you sure you really remembered what happened?" he finally said. "I mean, you're still here, aren't you? So she must have helped you out in the end. Maybe you fell in the water and at first your mother couldn't help you, because she was paralyzed by shock. Your imagination could've made up the rest."

"No, that's not how it was. You didn't see her eyes. She looked the way somebody looks who's doing something they have to do, but they almost can't bear it. Do you know what I mean? It's like she wanted to get me away from some awful danger — either real or imagined, I don't know. The point is, she chose a totally crazy way to do it."

Chloe wiped at her tears again. "Anna told me my mother was mentally ill, but what she didn't tell me was what my mother had done to me. I'm *sure* I'm right about this, Danny. Why do you think they put her in a hospital?"

"Look, so maybe she went to a hospital. Lots of people have emotional problems. Just because someone has a mental illness doesn't mean she'd try to hurt you."

Chloe shook her head. He was trying to comfort her — or himself. "Face it, Danny. Whatever it was, her sickness must have been really serious. It might — might even be the sort of thing I could inherit. It means that I don't know how *I'm* going to turn out."

Danny shrugged. "Who does?"

"I just don't understand it," she went on, as if she hadn't heard him. "My mother and Anna were identical twins, and Anna's normal. At least, I think she is, isn't she?"

"Yeah . . . " Danny said.

Chloe eyed him. The way he had said it surprised her. "What's wrong?" she asked. "I thought you liked Anna."

"I do," he said. "But since Mrs. Bass came to live here, Miss Kenyon's changed. If you see her in town with Mrs. Bass, she hardly speaks three words to you. And if she looks like she wants to talk, Mrs. B. grabs her arm and says they're in a hurry. Like she's afraid to let her talk to anyone. And yet when Miss Kenyon's on her own she's as friendly as anything. Most folks say she's moody, but I don't buy that."

"Anna's not moody," Chloe said. "I should know. I'm staying with her. She's kind of nervous, and sometimes her mind seems to be on other things, but she's not moody."

"Right," Danny agreed. "It's more as if she has to do what Mrs. Bass says. Like Mrs. Bass has something on her — you know, something Anna doesn't want people to know about — and Mrs. B. is kind of blackmailing her." He picked up his saw and began to cut off one end of the log. "You know, Chloe, it's sort of odd that your mother's body was never found."

"Danny!" she cried, horrified. "What are you saying? That my mother *didn't t*ake her own life? That someone murdered her? You *can't* think that Anna — "

Danny held up both hands and his face turned brick red. "No. Of course not."

"Well, what then?"

"Just that Miss Kenyon's been acting really odd lately, and I think it has something to do with Mrs. Bass."

Chloe shook her head. "You know, I kind of wondered last night if it was Anna I remembered standing over me, not my mother. I mean, they're so alike, aren't they? I might have mistaken her for my mother."

"Forget it, Chloe. Anna wouldn't hurt a fly. I was

thinking aloud, that's all. What I don't get is what Mrs. Bass is up to."

"Hey, I just remembered," Chloe said. "Mrs. Bass was creeping around her cottage last night. I heard her when I was lying on the beach — after I'd finally made it out of the lake."

Danny's head jerked up. "Did you actually see her?"

"No. Anna came along and, well, there was too much other stuff on my mind."

"So it might have been someone else you heard — Anna maybe?"

Chloe shook her head. "I don't see how it could have been. Anna was on the beach, looking for me."

"Any other ideas who it might have been?" He waited, watching her face with narrowed eyes.

Frowning, Chloe shook her head. "No. None. Gran wouldn't be walking around alone at night. She's too afraid of falling."

"You're sure it was Mrs. Bass?"

"No, not sure at all. Just that it might have been," Chloe said. "But no, wait. I forgot — she went back to Vancouver. She was only here a few hours. To pick up something for her show. The other day Anna said Mrs. Bass was going and later I heard her van drive away. And the van wasn't around yesterday."

"But you heard *someone* last night." Danny was still frowning, thinking. "If it wasn't Mrs. Bass, who was it?"

"I don't know. I was too freaked out to pay much attention at the time. It could have been Anna I heard, I suppose. I don't remember the exact order of when things happened. Honestly, Danny, I don't see that it matters."

She could have added that compared with the discovery of what her mother had done, nothing much seemed to matter, but Danny obviously felt differently. "I really don't think anything sinister was happening," she went on. "Mrs. Bass just makes people suspicious because she's so unfriendly."

"Unless there really *is* an intruder around," Danny said. "The same one that broke into your Gran's house." His frown deepened. "Chloe, I think you should be careful. Until we know what's going on, stay away from that cottage."

They were silent for awhile, Danny sawing away at his logs, probably still worrying about Mrs. Bass.

Chloe watched him work. Was he really worried, or making a mystery out of nothing in some well-meaning attempt to keep her mind off her mother? His own mind, too, maybe. Did he really believe her mother hadn't tried to drown her, or was he only saying it to comfort her? There was one way to find out how he really felt about what she'd told him. She plunged in. "School starts next week," she said. "I have to decide whether to go home, or talk Anna into letting me stay here."

"I guess that's right." Danny, arranging another log, did not look at her.

Chloe frowned. She'd hoped he would immediately say, "I wish you'd stay," but he only studied the log as if it posed a bigger problem than her decision about leaving or staying.

Her heart sank. He didn't care if she went! Maybe he even wished she would. Who could blame him? Knowing her history, who would want anything to do with her? Anyone who knew about her mother would surely always be watching her, looking for signs of the mother's sickness to show up in the daughter.

But she'd thought Danny, at least, would still want her. She wanted to find a place to hide where she could howl and howl and never stop until there were no more howls left inside her. But not here. Not now. She still had some pride left.

Danny's head was down and he seemed totally absorbed by the piece of log in front of him. She wanted to make things easy for him. "Anna seems to think I should go home, and I guess I should," she said. "I've pretty well found out what I wanted to know, and I can make Dad tell me the rest."

"Umm . . . Mum could probably find you a bed — that is, if you wanted to stay here," Danny said. "You'd have to do a few chores for rent. I'm not trying to pressure you, of course." He was still studying the log.

And then Chloe saw how it was. Even if he did want her to stay, he wouldn't ask her. He wouldn't risk being hurt, not again, like she'd hurt him when he took her to his special beach. She was the one who would have to risk it. "Oh, Danny! I don't want to leave," she burst out. "I want to stay here with you."

Still solemn, he gazed up at her. "You really mean that?"

"I wouldn't say it if I didn't. You don't have to say anything. I know how you must feel about my mother . . . "

In two strides he was with her, his arms around her. "Who cares about your mother? You're the one I care about."

The down on his upper lip felt soft and his lips tasted warm and sweet. Eagerly she returned his kisses. She wanted to hold him close, never let him go. She loved him. She was sure of that now. Nothing else mattered.

He paused and looked into her face, his smile one of wonderment. "And I thought you were scared of me."

"Scared of you? Crazy guy!"

"Crazy about you," he said. "For awhile there, when I thought you were leaving . . . " His voice cracked and he kissed her again, slowly.

At the crunch of someone's feet on the gravel they drew apart. "Dad!" Danny muttered, releasing her. Quickly, tenderly, he brushed her cheek with his lips. "See you later," he whispered.

Chloe ran down the path to the beach, not because she was embarrassed to let Mr. Wickel see her and Danny together, but because, when you're sixteen years old, you can't spread your arms like the wings of a plane and yell at the top of your lungs like a little kid, which was what she really wanted to do. Running downhill was the closest thing.

On the beach she grew solemn again and walked slowly along the bay of the marina. The worry over what she might have inherited from her mother was still there, deep inside. Yet she could still feel how beautiful the lake was, how beautiful the mountains, and the trees. Danny didn't care about the kind of mother she'd had. If he was prepared to accept her, mother and all, surely she could accept herself.

She had found the truth she had come to find. Now she had to learn to live with it.

Chapter Eighteen

Chloe was passing Mrs. Bass's cottage when she caught a glimpse of Anna. Half hidden by the lilac hedge, Anna stood on the garden path, lost in thought.

Mrs. Bass must still be away in Vancouver, Chloe decided, so Anna had come to check the cottage again this morning. Since the night of the mysterious intruder, she'd sure been conscientious about it.

"Anna," Chloe called.

Would Anna let her stay and go to school here? If not, Chloe would do as Danny had suggested and ask Marg, though she could guess that that idea would meet with some opposition from both Anna and Dad. Her dad hadn't replied to her letter yet, but she could always phone him. She didn't really want to talk to him because he'd just give her an argument, but still . . . Eager to get the matter settled, she turned in at the cottage gate. "Anna?"

The click of the latch startled Anna out of her

reverie. "What are you doing here?" she cried, flustered. Then, recovering, she said, "Sorry. You took me by surprise. I wasn't expecting anyone."

"I didn't mean to startle you," Chloe said. "Sorry." She wondered what Anna would have to say about last night, but instead Anna gestured toward the cottage.

"You haven't seen inside the cottage yet, have you? Come on in." In the kitchen she made herself at home and poured a cup of coffee from a pot on the stove. "Can I offer you something to drink?" she asked.

"Nothing, thanks. Anna, I wanted to ask you something. It's about staying with you and Gran next year and going to school here. We talked about it before, but it wasn't really settled, and now time's running out and I need to get it decided. Would it be okay with you?" Chloe, watching Anna's face for a reaction, sensed that Anna did not look enthusiastic at the prospect — to put it mildly. It took her awhile to reply, but Chloe was used to that. Finally Anna's brow cleared and she said, "Let me think about it and we can talk about it later."

Chloe frowned. She didn't want to talk about it later. She wanted to do it now, but she mustn't seem rude — especially when she was asking a favour. To be polite, she turned her attention to the few stone sculptures haphazardly displayed around the cottage. "Mrs. Bass's sculptures are very good," she said. She didn't have to lie. Much as she hated to admit it, Mrs. Bass had talent.

"What do you think of this one?"

Chloe looked where Anna was pointing. It was a soft sculpture, a female figure with such a sense of whimsy that Chloe found it difficult to associate it with Mrs. Bass. "I'm sure cloth isn't as difficult a medium to work in as stone," she said, "but this really is the one I like best." Now perhaps Anna would come away and they could discuss her staying on next year.

"Thank you. It's mine. I sell quite a few."

Surprise temporarily put everything else out of Chloe's mind. She vaguely remembered Marg Wickel mentioning Mrs. Bass's soft sculptures and wondered, fleetingly, why Anna didn't sell her work under her own name. "I had no idea you did this kind of thing," she said. "I guess it explains why you and Mrs. Bass are friends." After she'd said it, she realized it was a tactless remark, but Anna let it pass.

"I planned to go for a sail this morning," she said. "Why don't you come with me? We can talk on the boat."

In Chloe's opinion, a boat wasn't the most convenient place for a serious conversation. And she hardly wanted to be back on the lake, after what had happened last night. "What about Gran?" she countered.

"I arranged for her to go on a trip with the Seniors. They won't be back for hours. Come on, Chloe, it will give us a chance to talk."

Maybe the prospect of a few hours of freedom had gone to Anna's head, Chloe thought. Her cautious mood had changed and she seemed unusually light-hearted and pleased with herself. Maybe Anna and Dr. Como really were in love . . . If so, maybe he wouldn't want an extra person hanging around Anna's house. That might explain why Anna had looked less than enthusiastic about having her stay . . . Yes, Chloe decided, *that* must be what Mrs. Bass had meant when she said, "You have to choose between them." In the circumstances, Mrs. Bass's advice to "Get rid of her" was no doubt sensible. But it wasn't a decision that suited Chloe. She'd have to persuade Anna that she would not get in the way.

"We used to take you sailing when you were little," Anna said. "We played Three Men in a Boat. I always had to be the baker and bring cookies."

Anna, Roz and Chloe . . . Three men in a boat . . . Chloe could almost picture the scene, the laughter. At least, until her mother got sick. She wished Anna would recall little things like that more often. If only she herself could remember them. Maybe those little, tender memories would help ease the pain of her mother's later behaviour. Funny she felt shy talking to Anna about it . . . and that Anna still hadn't asked her how she was after last night.

"Do come sailing, Chloe," Anna begged. "It would mean a lot to me."

All right, Chloe thought, Anna was trying to keep her mind off her troubles. That's what this look at the cottage and the offer of a boat ride were about. She'd play along. Maybe it even *would* *h*elp.

They walked across the beach to the boathouse. Instead of hanging above the water, the sailing dinghy was already afloat, tethered to a ring.

"Climb in," Anna said.

As the boat bobbed beneath her weight Chloe was already wishing she hadn't agreed to come. "Shouldn't we have life jackets?" she asked.

"Oh, they get in the way when you're sailing."

"And I don't have any suntan lotion," Chloe said.

"Never mind. The clouds will be our sunshades," Anna said dreamily. "Lovely, fluffy, white ones. We'll drift along under them like Victorian ladies out for a picnic."

Chloe raised her eyebrows. "Are you serious?" What had got into Anna? It *must* be love!

Anna rowed them out of the boathouse. Over the lake white clouds floated in a blue sky, but behind the mountains the sky looked grey as lead, as if the weather might change.

"Are you sure this is a good time to go?" Chloe asked.

"Couldn't be better. We need a strong wind."

Out on the lake Anna told Chloe to hold the tiller steady while she raised the sail. Chloe scanned the marina. The figures of Marg's cottagers on the beach looked small, the children playing at the edge of the water while their parents lounged around. There was no sign of Danny.

Having raised the sail, Anna took the tiller back. "You sit there." She pointed. "When I tell you, duck under the boom as it swings across and sit on the other side."

The wind filled the sail and the boat heeled over. Chloe clutched at the sides.

"Sit on the edge and lean out to balance the boat," Anna said. "You'll soon get the hang of it. Sailing gives you a wonderful feeling of freedom. The land pulls you down and makes a grub of you, but water holds you up, like air. Ask the birds. They'll tell you."

Chloe stared at her aunt. First the soft sculpture, now this fanciful stuff. This was a side of Anna she'd never seen before. But Anna was right. Cloud shadows sailed across the lake as though trying to outrun the dinghy. There was a wild beauty in the skimming boat and flying clouds. It would make a great subject for a painting. "Where are we going?" she asked.

"Up there." Anna pointed to the far end of the lake. "Through the narrows."

"That's a long way." Chloe's doubts trickled back into her mind. The wind was strengthening and the boat heeled over at an increasingly alarming angle. Her fingers ached with the effort of clinging to the sides. If she lost her grip she would fall overboard, left behind by the racing boat. Inwardly, she groaned. Every time she thought she'd conquered her fears, they came back to make a wimp of her. "The clouds are piling up," she said. "I think we should go back pretty soon."

"There's something I have to do first."

"What?"

"You'll see."

Chloe gripped the sides harder. For some reason, Anna's enigmatic answer added to her feeling of uneasiness.

"Duck!" Anna yelled suddenly. The boom swung over.

Chloe ducked and clambered onto the high side of the boat, opposite the wind-filled sail. A couple of minutes later Anna yelled for her to duck again. They sailed up the lake in short zigzags, with Chloe dodging from side to side. She was getting tired. Last night's ordeal had been exhausting, struggling againt the waves for what seemed like hours. She wasn't used to this.

She had no sooner settled herself for what seemed like the hundredth time than Anna brought the boat about again. The boom swung over. Just in time, Chloe saw it coming.

"Duck!" Anna's order came slightly too late.

Chloe was furious, fear and weariness adding to her anger. If she hadn't been alert, the boom would have caught her, sending her crashing into the water, possibly knocking her unconscious. "Are you crazy?" she yelled, glaring at Anna.

Anna smiled. It was not Anna's usual, half-apologetic smile. The expression in her eyes was different too — hard and bright, blue pools frozen over with thin ice.

"Whatever gave you that idea?" she answered. But there was a tone of mockery in her voice that did nothing to reassure Chloe.

Chloe recoiled. This was Anna, but not Anna. It was Anna transformed, as if she had taken off one costume and put on another. Heaven help me, Chloe thought. Danny was right. There *is* something wrong with Anna. Maybe she cracked up, like my mother, only it took longer to come out in her . . . Or did it? Maybe it was Anna who was sick all along! What if I only thought it was my mother who almost drowned me, because she and Anna were so alike? No wonder Dad was so against letting me come here. Panic threatened to seize Chloe, strangling the breath in her throat.

The little boat raced over the water. Anna was like a jockey whipping her steed at the end of a race, intent on getting as much speed as possible out of it, bringing the boat about without warning.

She's doing it on purpose, Chloe decided, trying to knock me off the boat and drown me. But no, that's totally bizarre. People commit murder at night, in lonely alleys, not on a day in late summer with the wind blowing through your hair and the boat dancing over the water like a live thing. How could I even think such a thing? Murder's committed by some weirdo in a fit of anger, not some middle-aged woman, your kindly aunt, for heaven's sake. Maybe Anna's just so intent on handling the boat, she forgets to warn me.

Once again Anna brought the boat about. Again, no warning. Chloe, alert for danger, ducked and felt the boom brush against her hair.

Her anger flared again. What if, as Danny suspected, Mrs. Bass had some kind of power over Anna and Anna had to do what she said? Was it really my mother who was sick? Or was it Anna herself? Mrs. Bass might know the answers to those questions . . . even be blackmailing Anna to keep her secret.

The ballooning sail dipped closer to the water. Chloe gripped the high side of the boat, her hands almost numb, her shoulders and arms aching. Her thoughts were in tumult, piling up like the clouds overhead.

But I *liked* Anna, Chloe's mind insisted. Right from the moment I first met her. How could I have been so wrong?

Her two pictures of Anna didn't fit. It was like looking through a microscope before you get it focussed, the specimen blurred. I need time to think this through, but there isn't any time.

"Lean out farther," Anna shouted.

Sure, Chloe thought, her breath now coming in sobs. Lean out farther so that one false move will have me overboard. Even if she isn't *trying* to drown me, at this rate she's going to end up doing it anyway.

Chloe tried to fight down her fear, arguing with herself. Today Anna was changed. That was for sure. Were there two sides to her personality: good and evil, healthy and sick? No matter, the results were about the same. There must be some way to make Anna come back to her usual, cautious self. Maybe get her talking more.

Chloe wanted to sound calm, but because of the wind she had to raise her voice. "I thought you liked me." To her dismay, her voice shook.

"I do," Anna shouted back. "I think you're cute. I'm going to make a soft sculpture that looks just like you. I'll do the hair exactly like yours. I'll give her a paint palette and make her an artist. Your drawings show a lot of talent. It will be something to remember you by when you've gone."

Chloe scowled. Did she mean gone as in gone home, or gone as in dead? Catlike, alert for any move of Anna's that suggested she would bring the boat about, and with it the boom, Chloe kept her eyes on Anna's hand on the tiller. The blurred image snapped into focus. "You're right-handed!" Chloe cried.

"No kidding."

"Anna's left-handed. You're not Anna!"

"I never said I was."

"Then you're . . . you're . . . " Chloe could not get the word out.

"Roz."

Chloe's mind registered a dozen facts with that one word. Roz. Her mother. Her mother was still alive . . . And Danny had guessed. That's why he'd talked about Roz's body never being found; why he'd warned Chloe to stay away from Mrs. Bass's cottage. He'd been trying to lead her to the same conclusion, but was afraid to lay it all out for her. And she'd been too thick to pick up the clues.

"But . . . you drowned."

"That's what I wanted them to think." Roz's voice was triumphant. "I couldn't stand that hospital. I'd have gone mad if I'd stayed there any longer. Anna and your father put me in there. Everyone was against me, even Mother. Once I got out, I figured the only way they'd stop looking for me was if I was dead, so I made it look that way."

"So you faked your suicide," Chloe cried, suddenly angry. "You didn't care how that made Anna, or anyone else, feel. And before that you tried to drown me. I was only a little girl. Didn't you understand what you were doing? Tell me the truth — honestly."

But Roz only gazed back at her, her eyes icy and expressionless.

Chapter Nineteen

Chloe waited for an answer, desperately trying to read the expression in her mother's eyes. She *had* to know the whole truth, and only her mother could tell her that.

Roz allowed the speed of the dinghy to slacken. "They wanted to take you away from me," she finally said.

"Who did?"

"Anna and Owen, of course. She'd always loved him. She wanted him for herself. And she wanted you. When we were children Anna always took my dollies. She said I didn't look after them properly. But I loved you, and I did try to take care of you. That's why I decided to send you under the water to live with Tom and Mrs. Doasyouwouldbedoneby. Do you remember her? I used to read to you about her. She was so kind to Tom, the little chimney sweep. And he had such a good time swimming about. I thought you'd be happy with her, and they wouldn't be able to get you."

Tom from *The Water Babies* again. No wonder Anna hated the story so much. But you couldn't blame the book for Roz's disturbed mind taking the story and making it her reality. Chloe hoped that, after all these years, her mother's mind wasn't stuck in the same old groove, but listening to her was like having a dream, a kind of *Alice in Wonderland* nightmare, where people said things that sounded as if they made sense, but didn't.

Roz brought the dinghy about on another tack.

Just in time Chloe saw the boom coming and ducked under. "Look out!" she cried. "You'll knock me off the boat."

Her mother didn't answer. There's no use appealing to reason, Chloe decided. She'd try sympathy.

"I don't blame you for doing what you did," she said. "I know you were trying to do the best for me. But I'm not a little girl anymore. I'm too old to be a water baby. Besides, I don't want to live under the water with Tom. I want to live here — with you, my mother."

"I haven't been your mother for a long time," Roz replied. "Owen married again. But not Anna. Poor Anna. He took you away from her, too, didn't he? What a nasty shock." She looked smug, but her expression changed. "Anna wants you around more than she wants me — her own twin. Can you believe that?" As her sarcasm turned to anger, Roz sailed closer to the wind and the boat heeled over again. "As far as Anna's concerned I'm in the way now. But I'm not going back to that hospital, or some fancy nursing home, or anywhere else! Not for anybody, even you."

Roz looked like the stray cat gone wild that Chloe had once found and tried to tame. But terror had turned it vicious. It had twisted and turned, bit and clawed at her, prepared to kill to defend its freedom.

"No," Roz went on, "I'm sorry, but you've got to go."

"Go where? You mean, go back home?"

Ignoring Chloe's question, Roz concentrated on sailing.

"Listen," Chloe said. "You don't have to leave here on my account." She had to yell over the wind, and instead of sounding reassuringly confident, fear made her voice high and squeaky. "I'll go home to Edmonton. I won't tell anyone about you. Honest! I'll talk to Anna and tell her to let you stay."

"Anna would never go for it," Roz said. "She'd blame me for sending you away, and make me go instead."

Of course! Now Chloe understood. The choice Mrs. Bass had given Anna was not between Chloe and Dr. Como, but between Chloe and Roz.

"For a whole year I've either stayed out of sight, or pretended to be Anna," Roz said. "I've kept my side of the bargain, but Anna still wants to send me back to hospital." She looked about her like a hunted thing.

Without warning the boom came crashing over again. Just in time, Chloe ducked. Her apprehension grew. Her mother inhabited some unknown territory, full of frightening places where a stranger might put her foot wrong. No doubt about it. Her fears made her dangerous.

By now, thick clouds obscured the sun. The turtle-like houseboats that usually plodded around the edges of the lake had taken shelter and disappeared from view. There were no fountains of spray from power boats roaring across the water. The lake was one vast, empty expanse of grey waves.

Chloe tried again. "Please listen to me. I've been looking for you. That's why I came here. I couldn't remember you and I wanted to know what you were like. Now that I've found you, can't we get to know one another?" No response. "You're my mother. I won't let anybody send you back to the hospital."

"You can't stop them. You're only a girl. They won't listen to you."

I can't reach her, Chloe thought. Desperate, she tried to see where the life jackets were stowed, but there was no sign of them. Her arms trembled from the strain of hanging on. Her legs felt weak. To make matters worse, she seemed to have pulled a stomach muscle and every dodge under the boom was agony. How much longer could she hold out? If only another boat would come within hailing distance. Then she would let herself go overboard and trust the other boaters to pick her up. Willing something to appear, she scanned the horizon for other boats. Nothing.

Talking, as long as it didn't make Roz angry, seemed to slow her down a little. It was the only thing Chloe could think of doing, anyway. "You convinced everyone you'd drowned," she said. "That was really something. I don't know how you did it."

Roz's hunted expression vanished and she cheerfully called out over the noise of the rising wind. "It wasn't too hard. I was always a strong swimmer. I stashed some clean clothes on the shore, left the ones I was wearing on the boat, and swam for it. I did it at night, in the dark. You've no idea how exciting it was."

"But where have you been hiding all these years? I mean before you came back here."

For a moment Roz didn't answer, then she shrugged. "Oh well, what harm can it do to tell you? I worked on a ranch in the interior. After I'd 'drowned,' I hitched a ride with a cowboy. I told the rancher someone had stolen all my papers and he gave me a job. I've always liked working with horses. You're freer, out on the range. But it was hard to be so far from water . . . "

Chloe couldn't think of anything to say. She scanned the lake. Still no sign of another boat. Where were they all? She'd have to keep Roz talking. "You were safe at the ranch. Why did you came back here?"

"I told you. I love to sail and I missed the lake," Roz said. "Anna nearly died of shock when I turned up on the doorstep. I talked her into letting me live in the cottage. Why should she live here on the lake, and not me?"

"You've been living in the cottage? What about Mrs. Bass?"

"Mrs Bass is a spy. Anna says she's a nurse, but I don't believe that. But Bassy has her uses. Anna and I were always good at pretending to be one another, and Bassy coordinates things. You see, we can't appear in two places at the same time, and we always have to do our hair the same way and all that."

"Mrs. Bass doesn't let you talk to anyone very much, so you won't give yourself away. That's right, isn't it?" The picture in Chloe's mind was coming clear. "But you can't go on this way, you know. People will get suspicious." There was still a chance she could make her mother see reason.

"Things were fine until *you* showed up," Roz said, turning sulky. "Then it was out to Vancouver with me. 'Just a little holiday,' Anna said. She thinks I'm stupid. All the people in that 'hotel' she sent me to were crazy. So I gave Bassy the slip and came back."

"And that's when you crept into Gran's house and I almost caught you."

"Like heck you did. You screamed so loud you almost frightened me to death. After that, Bassy dragged me away again. The old sleeping pill in the cocoa trick. I'm so tired of riding in the back of that van. Can't see a thing. Of course, I only pretended to drink the next cocoa she gave me. Then I fixed *her* bedtime drink — guess what I put in that? — and took the next bus home." While she talked, Roz continued to take the dinghy on a long, swift tack up the lake.

Chloe was wet and cold. She could scarcely feel

the boat. Her hands cleaved to its edge, frozen to its shape. She felt totally helpless. She tried not to look down. The water rushing by could easily make her dizzy. She might lose her balance and fall in.

The wind was whipping up the water and it was getting harder to see the rest of the lake. Still, she mustn't give up hope. A power boat could still catch up with them. Until one did, she had to try to sound understanding. Not put her mother on the defensive. Her mother lived in a different world, a world of fear and suspicion where even your identical twin and your own child threatened your safety, where the rules of the real world didn't count. How could you reach someone like that?

Again Roz brought the dinghy about. The little boat seemed to take a deep breath before leaping forward. Lightning forked over the headlands that squeezed the lake into the narrow passage Roz was aiming for.

Chloe stared at the looming cliffs. Her mother was being so reckless she might fail to negotiate the gap. Chloe's heart banged madly against her chest as if it were trying to escape from a locked room. "Stop!" she screamed as the boat sped faster toward the cliffs. "You'll run into the headlands and we'll both be killed."

"Don't be such a wimp," Roz called over the wind. "This is exciting. So what if we drown? Drowning isn't a bad way to die."

Chloe felt as if the whole world had gone mad. She watched as the mouth of the narrows waited to swallow them up. Once inside she might be able to swim as far as land, but there were no beaches to be seen, only steep slopes running down into the water.

As Chloe's mind whirled, wind rushed around her head. The gale came from a new direction, tearing at her hair. Overhead, lightning forked.

The flash was the last thing she remembered before the world became a chaotic place of noise and pain and tilting horizons.

A sudden silence surprised her. She was underwater. Automatically, she kicked madly for the surface. Her head ached unbearably. She pressed her hand against her eyes in an effort to clear her vision. Dimly, she saw the dinghy overturned, its sail submerged.

Don't panic, she told herself. Keep your head. She repeated it over and over, to keep herself calm. She began to tread water and try to breathe without hyperventilating. Her head throbbed as if someone had smashed it. Maybe someone had. Where was her mother? If only everything wouldn't keep going black . . . If only she could reach the dinghy . . . Every lift of her arm sent a stab of pain through her head.

Back in Edmonton, she'd practiced righting a boat in the pool, but that was a canoe, not a sailboat with a submerged sail. Besides, she was in too much pain now even to attempt it.

Where was her mother? No sign of her. Clawing at the hull, Chloe tried to haul herself out of the water. The effort sent bursts of pain through her head, blinding her. Waves of nausea sickened her. She fell back.

Then her mother was behind her. The feel of her mother's arms gripping her legs was the last thing she remembered before she passed out.

When she came to it took her awhile to realize where she was. Not in the water. Below her the surface was hard. Cautiously she raised her head, then quickly lowered it because of the pain. She was lying on the hull of the boat. Where was her mother now?

Don't worry about her, warned her inner voice. *If you pull her up here with you, she might push you off.* But I can't just leave her, Chloe thought. Whatever happens, she's my mother.

Moving set the hammers going again in her head. Clenching her teeth, she lay on her stomach across the hull and scanned all around the boat. There was no sign of her mother.

A lightning flash lit up the water. Almost simultaneously there was a terrible crack — as though the world had split open. Chloe screamed and covered her head with her arms. When she dared look up again she realized that the scene shown by the lightning flash seemed to have been printed on her retina. She recalled it as easily as if she could still see it. Her mother had been nowhere in sight. A single oar floated nearby. Could her mother have tried to swim to shore, using the other oar to help her?

Confused by dizziness and the pain in her head, Chloe tried to figure what might have happened to her mother. Would anybody survive long in the lake? It was late summer, the water warm . . . The storm had moved on, but the water was so dark and choppy, she couldn't see anything much. Even if her mother was quite close, she might not be visible. She strained to listen, hoping to hear her mother call out. If only her head didn't ache so blindingly. She felt so sleepy . . .

When she came to again, the wind and rain had chilled her to the bone. She shivered violently. She might be warmer in the water. But what if the lightning came back? Her aching head wrestled with the question of safety in an electrical storm. Where would she be safer — on the boat or in the water? She couldn't think.

All about her the world was dark, almost like night, lit only by distant lightning flashes. She felt so tired. It would be best not to sleep. She would close her eyes, but only for a minute.

"Chloe!" Danny's voice. He must have come calling for her. "Wake up, Chloe. Catch the rope."

Confused, she tried to sit up, but her body wouldn't obey. Someone was dragging her, none too gently. She was lying on something very hard and uncomfortable. She wanted to ask where she was, but she was too tired.

Danny knelt beside her, his face almost touching hers. "Was anyone else on the boat with you?" He asked. "Chloe, think! It's important."

"My mother," she whispered. "Please find my mother."

"Okay. Don't talk anymore. You're going to be okay."

Chapter Twenty

After a day of worrying, plus X-rays and a battery of tests, Chloe managed to sleep, even though her mind kept going back to the boat, the storm, the scene with her mother.

Soon after she woke up Anna and Dr. Como came to see her. One look at Anna's face told Chloe the news she did not want to hear. Her mother's body had been found.

"I've just been to identify her," Anna said, her voice breaking.

Chloe reached for Anna's hand. No wonder Anna looked close to collapse. Yet, watching her, Chloe could think of nothing comforting to say. It was as if someone had anaesthetized her feelings.

After Dr. Como took Anna home to rest, Chloe lay back on her pillows, eyes closed, thinking. She must have drifted off to sleep, because the next thing she knew was that someone was holding her hand.

"How are you feeling now, girl?"

Girl? Girl was what Dad called her when he felt tender. It was a bit of the left-over Welsh in him, he said. Chloe opened her eyes. "Dad! What are you doing here?"

He bent to kiss her. "Nice to see you, too, Chloe," he said.

She bit her tongue. Sarcasm — always her dad's defence when he was hurt. But she couldn't throw her arms around him the way she used to. There were too many unanswered questions between them.

"Anna phoned yesterday and told me what happened," he said. "So I drove straight here the moment I heard. I — I stopped at Anna's just before I came to the hospital and she — " He closed his eyes for a moment. "She told me they'd found Roz's — your mother's — body."

Chloe tried to read what was behind his voice. There were bags under his eyes and his face sagged. Then he seemed to pull himself together. "The doctor phoned Anna's just as I was leaving. He says you can go home today."

Which home? "You got my letter?" Chloe asked.

He nodded. "We miss you, Joyce and I, and the boys. They're always asking when you're coming home. Nearly drive us mad, the pair of them."

How like him not to ask her straight out to forget the letter and come home. He came at things sideways. This time, Chloe was glad. It meant she didn't have to give him a straight reply — not yet. He searched her face. Finding no answer to his silent plea, he sighed.

"If they're letting me out I'll need some clothes," she said. "The ones I was wearing when I came in here are a write-off."

Owen nodded at the zippered bag at his feet. "I brought some." Seeing her horrified expression he said, "Don't worry. Anna picked them out."

So he and Anna must have patched up their differences. About time.

He left the room to talk to the doctor one more time. When he got back, Chloe was dressed. "Ready, Chl— Where did you get *that?*" he asked, staring at her mother's necklace.

"Anna gave it to me. She must've tucked it into the bag for me. It's the only thing I have left of my mother's now." As she fingered the necklace, tears sprang to her eyes.

He nodded and said no more. Then he took her arm and silently led her to his car.

"We have to talk," Chloe said when they'd been in the car for almost ten minutes and neither of them had said a word.

"Okay. I thought we'd stop at Margaret Falls. It should be quiet this late in the season." He drove into the empty parking lot. "Feel up to a walk, or are you too groggy?"

"Maybe a short walk. I could use some fresh air." It might help clear the foggy feeling in her head.

A footpath to the falls ran alongside the stream that flowed through the small canyon.

"Pretty spot, isn't it?" Owen said. "Your mother and I used to come here when we were young. We brought you a few times." He sounded stiff and unnatural, as though it was difficult for him to bring up the subject of her mother.

On the walls of the canyon, thin evergreens struggled to keep a footing. Falling, some of them had tumbled down to the canyon floor where, covered in moss, they lay every which way. Others kept barely a toe-hold, their roots exposed, their trunks leaning out at crazy angles. A few twisted trunks, supported by metal stands to prevent them from falling right across the path, arched over it.

"I don't think it's pretty," Chloe said. "It reminds me of one of those gloomy Victorian oil paintings. The artist would probably call it Grotto of Lost Souls, or something like that."

"Maybe pretty is the wrong word," Owen agreed. "But it appeals to most people, I think. There's a fairy story feel about it — you know, the forest under a magic spell, waiting to wake up, and all that Sleeping Beauty stuff."

They reached the falls, a chute of water plunging into a rock-lined pool. The pool was not deep and only partly surrounded by a rail fence. They leaned their elbows on the top rail and watched the water fall into the pool.

"Dad, I didn't come to admire the scenery," Chloe said. "I want to know why you never told me about my mother."

"I'm sorry, love. Anna told me you know about your mother's illness. That was bound to come as a shock."

"Not as much of a shock as *meeting* her after thinking she'd been dead all those years. And then the storm, the — " Chloe couldn't go on. Her father put a hand on her arm, and her anger flared again. "Why didn't you marry Anna after my mother supposedly committed suicide?" she said. "According to Gran, Anna always loved you."

Owen straightened up and gripped the rail. "Maybe she did, Chloe, but I didn't love *her*."

"Why not? She was my mother's identical twin."

"Identical twins aren't clones. They're individuals. Don't ask me why I loved one twin and not the other. I don't know."

"I don't believe you. When we were on the boat together, my mother said you and Anna were in love. No wonder she went crazy." Chloe didn't even try to keep the blame out of her voice.

Owen turned pale. "Unfortunately, she wrote the same thing in her 'suicide' note — by way of revenge on Anna and me, I suppose. I know she didn't want to go into the hospital, but it was the only thing that might have helped her. Anyway, her accusation hurt me more than you can know — oh, not only because it gave me some trouble with the police, but because it wasn't true. I'd always loved her and only her. After she died, all I knew was that I had to forget her, and my feelings of bitterness, and make a new life for you and me. How could I do that if every time I looked at Anna, I saw Roz?"

But now that Chloe had started blaming him, she couldn't stop. "So you ran off with me without saying anything to Anna. Nothing at all!"

"I'm not proud of what I did, Chloe. But think

what I'd been through. First your mother's illness and having to put her in hospital and see her desperately unhappy; then her supposed suicide and all the heartache associated with that. When Anna suggested we marry and make a home for you, I knew I had to refuse her, and I couldn't take any more emotional upheavals. It was easier to run away. Afterwards, when I'd recovered my senses a little, I wrote to Anna and told her you were okay. Every year I wrote to her through a lawyer and told her how you were doing and sent photos."

"But until a few months ago, you never gave me her replies. You let me think my relatives didn't want to have anything to do with me. That was cruel — to them and to me." A dry sob shuddered in Chloe's throat, surprising her.

Owen rubbed his forehead as though it ached. "Perhaps it was. But you seemed to have forgotten your mother and everything about this place. I thought it best to leave it that way."

Chloe was like a boxer with his opponent on the ropes. She couldn't rest until she had delivered the knock-out blow. "Why didn't you tell me my mother tried to drown me when I was a little girl?" she demanded.

As though reeling from a punch, Owen took a step back from the rail. "Who told you that?"

"Nobody. I finally remembered."

"Now do you see why I didn't want you to come?" he cried. "I was afraid that something, or someone, Gran or Anna maybe, or even the lake, would trigger a memory. Or someone, a stranger even, might say something. Can't you see? I didn't want you to know."

"It was worse *not* to know," Chloe shot back. She wished she didn't have to cry. She felt angry, not sad. "If only you'd told me about the ordinary things — like you did just now when you said you both used to bring me here — I mightn't have got so screwed up about her. I thought I'd killed her, for heaven's sake. You should have told me the truth — all of it."

"How do you tell a child a thing like that?" he cried. "Your mother was sick. Chloe, try to understand. She didn't know what she was doing."

"I do understand. Anna told me about her sickness, but not that she'd tried to drown me. Nobody wanted to tell me that." Angrily, she wiped her eyes with her jacket sleeve. "So how come I made it to sixteen anyway? How come I'm still alive? Did my mother suddenly realize what she was doing, and stop? Why didn't I drown back then?"

"Anna and I were nearby, working on Roz's sailboat. By that time we had realized Roz was sick, so we tried never to leave you alone with her. We heard you cry out. I don't remember who got there first. Anna worked on reviving you while I held onto your mother. She fought like a wildcat. I don't know what she thought we were doing to you, but obviously she was terrified. Poor, confused Roz." He leaned his elbows on the rail and held his head, staring into the pool. "For awhile Anna and I wondered if you were going to make it. It's not a scene I care to re-live."

Chloe, watching him suffer, wondered why she couldn't stop feeling angry with him.

He stood up and turned to look at her. "My God, Chloe, if I'd known Roz was still alive . . . and around here. When I think what might have happened . . . Tell me, girl," he said urgently, his eyes searching her face, "the boat capsizing, your concussion. Was it really all an accident? What really happened out there?"

She told him the truth, exactly as she had told Anna. " . . . but at the end, when my mother had the chance to drown me, or simply leave me to drown, she didn't. In fact, I think she probably saved my life." Thinking of it brought new tears to Chloe's eyes.

Calmer now, Owen found a tissue in his pocket and handed it to her. "I think she probably *did* save you. It might be hard to believe, but she always loved you."

"That's what she said when we were on the boat," Chloe said, sobbing. "But she had a strange way of showing it."

"Chloe, try to see things from her point of view," Owen said. "A little while ago you said you didn't like this place." He looked around. "I can see why. To us, this isn't normal. But your mother saw things differently. It's as if, in her mind, trees naturally grew sideways out of the hill instead of straight up; and their roots were always exposed to the air instead of being planted firmly in the ground. D'you see? Her mind played tricks on her. She saw unusual things as normal, and the other way around, so she ended up not knowing when she was doing the wrong thing. I wish I could explain it more clearly."

"You don't have to. I know what you mean," Chloe said. "To my mother, sending me to live with the water babies was some kind of gift. Not a danger. It was her way of loving me." She wished she could stop crying. Her tissue was sodden now, totally useless.

Owen sighed heavily. "Love is a powerful emotion. Unfortunately, it doesn't come with a set of blueprints for doing the right thing, and you don't have to be sick to be misguided by it. Just now you told me I was wrong to hide the truth from you. But girl, I did it because I love you."

"You were *wrong!*" She started down the path, away from him. Her injured head ached unbearably. Blinded by the pain, she hit her head against one of the branches that hung over the trail. She stopped cold, crying. Gently Owen led her to a bench beside the path and lowered her onto it.

"It's not fair," Chloe cried. "Just when I found my mother, she had to die. Now I'll never get to know her. Anna should have told me she was alive. If only she'd let us meet. If only I could have got to know her." Too many "if onlys" kept playing in her mind — round and round like an endless recording.

"I know, love. I know." Her father gathered her to him and let her cry against his shoulder. "From now on, I'll do my best to fill in the gaps. If you'll only give me the chance."

He rubbed her back, the way he used to when

she was a little girl. "Try not to blame Anna. She was only trying to protect you, because she loves you too." He let her have her cry and then said, "Come on, love, we'd better go back to Anna and Gran. I've got a few years' worth of apologizing to do."

When they got back, Gran was in the kitchen. Beside her stood the tea trolley which had once been immobilized and used as a plant stand for African violets. Gran had restored it to its original purpose and set out cups and saucers, creamer and sugar bowl, complete with silver teaspoons and cloth napkins.

"Chloe, my dear, it's so good to see you," Gran cried. "Are you fully recovered? My dear child, your eyes are red. Have you been crying?"

"I'm okay now, really, Gran." After they had hugged, she said. "The tea cart looks lovely. Can I help?"

"Well, since you're kind enough to offer, perhaps you would fill the teapot. A full kettle is a bit heavy for my shaky hands. Wait now. Let it come to a full boil." As though she'd seen Owen only yesterday, Gran turned to him and said, "Go and join the others in Anna's bedroom. She's lying down. I thought everybody could use a nice cup of tea."

Then to Chloe, she said, "Anna is in a real state. The police were here this morning, you know. Roz's body has been found. Poor Anna had to identify her. I don't know why Owen couldn't have done it."

Chloe put her arm around her grandmother.

Time, dodging through the years, was still playing tricks on Gran, mixing up past and present. "Come on, Gran," she said. "It's time to have our tea."

Chapter Twenty-One

Later in the day, after she had had a nap, Chloe phoned Danny.

"Hey, Chloe," he said. "How're you feeling?"

"Okay. As long as I remember not to move my head too fast."

"I tried to visit you in the hospital, but they said family only, because you had to rest."

"I'm sorry, Danny," Chloe said. "I don't know how to thank you for rescuing me. Just saying thank you doesn't seem to do it. I probably owe you my life."

"No problem."

"Listen, I'm supposed to take things easy for the next few days, but I think I can talk Dad and Anna into letting me go to our special beach tomorrow — just for awhile. To — to talk . . . Say, about noon?"

"You've got it."

Next day, at the beach, they threw their towels onto the pebbles. Danny flopped down. Chloe took things more gently. If she moved too quickly, her head still ached.

"I expected you to be bandaged up like an Egyptian mummy," Danny said.

Chloe grimaced. "They shaved my head at the back so they could stitch up the cut. That's why I'm wearing a hat. They can't put a cracked skull in a cast. You just have to take painkillers and wait for it to heal."

She knew he must be curious about what had happened to her on the lake, but she wasn't sure she could talk about her mother without breaking down, and she'd done enough of that yesterday, so she continued to avoid the subject.

"Danny, I meant it when I said I probably owe you my life."

He blushed. "No way! I'm sorry I took so long finding you, but when it started to rain it was hard to see anything out there."

"How did you even know I was out on the lake?"

"Anna phoned me to ask for you. You'd left her a note, remember? You'd had lots of time to get home from our place so I began to worry. I suspected something weird was going on. You know how I felt about Mrs. Bass, except it wasn't only Mrs. Bass I couldn't figure out. There was Anna, too. The first thing I did was check the cottage. No one was home, but it looked like someone had been there recently, and Buck was racing around with his nose to the ground. He kept running to the boathouse and whining. By that time Anna was pretty frantic about you, so I asked her straight out if her sister was still alive. She admitted it right away. We checked the boathouse and saw the dinghy was gone. The rest was easy. Dad took one boat and I took mine, and Anna phoned the lake police. She didn't have to. We wouldn't have said anything to get her into trouble, but she said we needed all the help we could get to find you. She was pretty scared, I can tell you."

Chloe nodded. "The police came to the hospital to ask me what happened."

"What did you tell them?"

"The truth. That I went sailing with my mother thinking she was Anna, and she told me on the boat who she really was. When we got into the narrows the wind suddenly blew from another direction and the boat went over. I suppose I hit my head on something, because I tried to climb onto the hull, but kept passing out. When I came to, that's where I was. My mother must have boosted me up, but there was no sign of her."

She hadn't told the police that her mother's behaviour on the boat had frightened her. Somehow it didn't seem like any of their business. It was something just between her and her mother.

I haven't told Danny the whole truth, either, she thought. But, when you got down to it, what *was* the whole truth? On the boat it had been easy to think of Roz and Anna as two halves of the same person — one evil, one good; one sick, one healthy. But nobody was that simple. If a freak wind hadn't taken Roz by surprise, what would she have done?

"Why can't the cops leave you alone for now?"

Danny asked. "I mean, it's bad enough losing your mother twice over, without them bothering you."

The concern in his voice almost brought her to tears. "It's worse for Anna," she said, sniffing. "The detective who interviewed her said she should have reported my mother's whereabouts to the police. He sort of accused her of playing games. But it wasn't a game to Anna. Hiding my mother was a terrible strain on her. No wonder she always seemed so jumpy."

"Why did she do it?" Danny asked. "I mean, for such a smart woman it was kind of a dumb thing to do. I never would have told on her, but sooner or later other people beside me would have guessed the truth. What was in it for her, anyway?"

"Nothing. But she knew how afraid my mother was of being cooped up in an institution." Chloe could understand Anna's reluctance to go against Roz's wishes. The memory of her mother's terror was still vivid in her mind. She knew what a terrible thing fear was, and truly pitied her mother for having to live with it. If only she could have found a way to comfort her. But she hadn't.

Danny didn't try to rush her. When she was able to go on, she said, "Anna really did love my mother. I think she felt guilty, too. Of course it wasn't her fault, but she must have asked herself why her twin got sick, and she didn't. Maybe she felt she had to make up in some way for the unfairness of their lives. And I do think Anna had always been under my mother's thumb. Gran thought so. I suppose it was a kind of habit. My mother wouldn't *let* Anna tell me she was alive."

"But in the end your mother's curiosity got the better of her," Danny said. "First she sneaked a look at your drawings, then she tricked you into thinking she was Anna so she could go out in the boat with you and see what you were like."

"D'you think so?" There might be some truth in Danny's explanation. Chloe gazed out over blue water and blue sky. Today it was hard to believe there had ever been a storm. "If only I wasn't such a wimp."

"What are you talking about?"

"If I hadn't passed out, I might have saved her. I could have given her a hand and helped her climb onto the hull too. She'd still be alive."

Danny sat up and glared at her. "Enough of the guilt trip. Nobody can just decide to ignore getting hit on the head. You are definitely not a wimp, Chloe, but there are times when you are pretty stupid."

"Thanks for the compliment," she said. But his anger amused her enough to stop another flow of tears.

"Look," he said, touching her hand. "I don't want to sound unfeeling, but if your mother had lived, she wouldn't have had a very happy life, would she? She'd have had to go back to that hospital, whether she wanted to, or not. Maybe fate's been kinder this way."

"Anna said she went on hiding my mother in the hope that someone would discover a new medicine, or some new treatment, that would help. Maybe not a cure, but something to keep her closer in touch with reality. Then she could have talked my mother into confessing to the authorities and helped her build a new life. Now, even if they find some cure tomorrow, it will be too late."

Danny squeezed her hand. "I'm sorry. I guess I hadn't thought of that."

His hand felt warm and strong — reassuringly alive and human. Chloe wished she didn't have to let go of his hand, ever.

But she did. There was no easy way to tell him. Better to do it quickly, before she had second thoughts. "Danny, I'm going back to Edmonton with my dad."

"What?" He stared at her. His colour rose. "But the other day you said . . . "

She couldn't bear to see the hurt in his eyes. "I know, and I still mean it — the way I feel about you — but a lot's happened since then."

"Nothing that affects us." He rolled over onto his back and stared moodily at the sky. "Oh, I get it. Your dad's been talking to you. I thought he would. Yesterday evening he was over at our place, asking me and my parents about school here. He seems to think it's some kind of mindless bog compared to what you have in Edmonton."

"That's not it."

"What then?" He sounded angry.

"I like you too much."

He sat up and stared at her. "There are times when you just don't make sense. How can it be possible to like someone too much?"

"It was something Dad said about love not coming with instructions. Wonderful as it is, it doesn't necessarily tell us the smartest thing to do. I *want* to stay here with you, Danny, with all my heart, but I need time to sort myself out. Dad and I need time to work things out, too. Having Joyce and the little kids around will help. Joyce is so straightforward, and sensible. I need my family, Danny. If I stayed here, I'd be tempted to lean on you, use you as a kind of security blanket, and I don't want it to be that way. It wouldn't be, well, normal. D'you understand?"

"You're trying to say you don't want a shrink and a boyfriend in the same package?"

She leaned over and gently kissed him. For awhile there was no one else in the world but Danny. How could she leave him? To comfort herself as much as him, she thought of the times they could be together.

"I'll be back every holiday, Danny. And if you and I really care for one another, our feelings won't change just because we're apart."

"Mine won't." Leaning on his elbow, Danny moodily played with the pebbles. "Trouble is, you meet loads of guys — all the activities you've got going. You're bound to find someone else."

She watched him, his eyelashes thick against his tanned cheek, and her breath caught in her throat. She made an effort to steady her voice and sound as if she were teasing. "So might you."

He looked up with a wry grin. "Yeah!" he said. "Maybe I will at that."

And suddenly she knew it was going to be all right. Sure, his feelings might change. People's feelings did, sometimes. But not overnight. Definitely not because some other girl told him he was cute.

"Jerk," she said, laughing. "You're mine, Danny Wickel, and don't you forget it, or you'll be sorry."

Flinging a handful of pebbles at him, she leaped up. Too fast! Momentarily dizzy she staggered. Danny grabbed for her ankle and missed. Chloe, screaming in mock terror, flung herself into the water with Danny hollering wildly in her wake.